Possessed by You

ALICIA MARINO

Possessed by You

First Print Edition: June 2019

Limitless Publishing, LLC
Kailua, HI 96734
www.limitlesspublishing.com

Formatting: Limitless Publishing

ISBN-13: 978-1-64034-616-1
ISBN-10: 1-64034-616-3

Dedication

To my favorite two women on the planet—my conquering mom and remarkable sister—thank you.

CHAPTER ONE

"Well, Miss *Fontaine*, you're finally reborn. You can leave all that past bullshit far behind you." Kevin grins, slinging a strong arm around my shoulder as we stride down the steep steps of the courthouse. It took more strength than I thought I had to enter the building and even more to request to permanently change my name for good. The love I have for my parents is strong, but the attachment to the man whose blood is on my hands outweighs the need to keep their name. I spent my time hiding and paying for circumstances that were forced upon me.

No more.

"So, where do you want to eat? We'll celebrate," Kevin persists after my long silence.

If this was a year ago, he and I would conquer the town, and I wouldn't feel an ounce of uncertainty. If this was a year ago, I'd still be naïve to harsh realities. Instead, my days are spent either face deep in work or trapped in memories of times I'd very much like to forget.

It makes it hard to celebrate something like this.

"I wish I could. I have to get some work in today."

"You're always working," he complains, glaring under light lashes.

"This job is kicking my ass," I gripe as Kevin reaches up to hail a cab. "But—"

"But you love it. I'm well aware." He grips the handle of the checkerboard door and slides onto the worn leather beside me. "I just miss you is all."

Knowing I'm constantly hot and cold, forcing him to endure my fluctuating temperatures, guilt supersedes my indifference.

"Look, we'll go out this week. We'll party like we're in our twenties."

"We *are* still in our twenties, Darcy."

"That's my point. We deserve a night to go a little crazy."

"Just us?"

It surprises me to hear that, considering he and Doug are nearly inseparable as of late. In the weeks that I've been reacquainting myself with the world, and with my man, I've definitely noticed that Kevin hardly sees his apartment anymore, and his talk of the opposite sex has ceased altogether. That can only mean one thing: commitment.

"Sure, yeah, it can be just us. Are you and Doug okay?"

"Yeah, we're fine. I just want some good old fun with my girl."

He circles his arm around my shoulder and squeezes. The city is abuzz outside. The infamous New York traffic is nearly at a standstill, the sidewalks crowded with businessmen and women. Vendors are parked on the corners of the blocks, and construction workers dangle along the new high rises that have magically appeared seemingly overnight.

"I've been seeing a lot of Ben in the papers lately," Kevin interjects into our peace.

"He's on a roll, expanded to nearly half the world now. He's in Taiwan at the moment."

"Christ, man. That's crazy. When do you even see him?"

"I see him plenty. He's returning Friday."

"And are you guys living together yet?"

I look down to contain my disappointment. "No, we agreed to wait a little bit for that."

Weeks ago, it felt wrong to just jump right back into his world. Moving in seemed to both of us like a leap into something we knew wasn't smart. I expected we'd devote our time to our relationship and eventually reach the place where we were before, when we couldn't go even one night apart.

That place hasn't been reached yet, to my everlasting worry.

He raises a sharp brow, pursing his lips. "Why? I think what you two need is close proximity right now. He shouldn't be on business trips, and you shouldn't be living at your desk."

I can always count on Kevin to never sugarcoat anything.

"It's just I was given this job, literally *given*, and I can't ask him to back away from his work either. He accomplished so much while I was…away. I can't ask that of him."

"You shouldn't have to," he mutters, shaking his head.

"Look, I know we've handled this whole situation terribly, but we're trying. We'll be okay."

***

My cell phone blares, buried deep under piles of paperwork. I rummage hopefully, anticipating a certain name on the screen. Relieved to find my hopes rewarded, I answer with a wide grin. "I miss you."

Benjamin's returning chuckle spreads throughout my body, ridding me of the discomfort that's followed like a shadow in my day. *"I miss you too, baby."*

"How are you? Where are you?"

"I'm on the jet."

"Wait, why? I thought you were in Taiwan till Friday?"

"I'm coming back early."

Benjamin, business extraordinaire and man on the rise, who lives to work, is cutting his trip short? Whether it's an overreaction or not, I begin to overthink.

"Is everything okay?"

"Everything's fine."

"It's unlike you to cancel a trip."

"I want to take you somewhere."

I stop swiveling in my chair and plant my feet, facing the wide window showcasing the illuminated buildings. "What?"

"Pick wherever you want, but we're leaving as

soon as I land."

"As much as I'd like to, Benjamin, I can't leave. I have work tomorrow."

"There are many perks of having a boyfriend that's friends with your boss."

"You spoke to Cindy?"

"Kevin too."

It's telling how fast my grin disappears. "Are you serious?"

"Of course I am."

"Right…well, is he making you do this?"

"You think I'd let Kevin make my decisions for me? No, he was upset, I will admit, and I let him know that he is not at all part of the relationship between you and me. However, everything he said were things I already knew. You and I could do with a pause, to evaluate…figure some things out."

I'm mortified. "Ben, I know you're busy. I don't want to take you from your work."

"No, you come first. Always. I told you that."

He's said that to me multiple times. I think we've lost that motto along the way somewhere. Our blinders have been up, and this conversation is the first time he's hinted that he wants to take them down. For that reason alone, this trip is suddenly of the utmost importance.

"When are you going to be here?"

"I'm about five hours away now, so I'll land late. Probably around one. Do you think you can stay awake until you're on the plane?"

"Yeah, I can." I pick up my purse from the desk.

"What's that noise?"

"I'm packing up."

"You're still at work?" He chuckles, and I imagine him shaking his head. *"Jesus, a few months in and you're staying late every night. Should I be nervous?"*

I smile, logging out of my computer. "It's only because you're not here to keep me entertained."

"Well, I look very much forward to entertaining you...I'll have Dimitri pick you up and take you to the plane. Think of where you want to go. Anywhere you'd like."

***

"Hi, Dimitri," I say, approaching the limo, eyes burning from lack of sleep. "Long time no see."

"Yes, I'm mainly behind closed doors now." He takes my luggage from me, which to my shame is heavy enough to weigh down even his beefy arm. With no clue where Benjamin plans to escape to, I had to improvise.

"Well, it's good to see you." I get in when he opens the back door for me, sliding onto the cool leather. It's a scorcher. Summers in New York can be absolutely brutal.

"You too, Miss Fontaine."

Exhausted, the minute he shuts the door behind me, my eyes become heavy. A soft voice is crooning from the radio in the front, drawing my eyes closed even faster. I re-open them when an arm comes around my back, another beneath the crook of my knees, lifting me off the seat. Delirious, I lean my head against Benjamin's chest as we make our way through the tarmac toward the jet.

"You don't have to carry me. I can walk."

"Have you thought of where you'd like to go?" He smiles down at me warmly, his jet black hair shining off the bright lights from the posts. Fifteen hours and he appears refreshed and excited. He steps carefully, ducking when he reaches the door.

"Anywhere you are is good with me," I mumble.

"All right, we're gassing up the plane now. We have to be in our seats for the takeoff, but you can sleep in the cabin after that."

I pout playfully, unable to keep my eyes open as he deposits me into a seat and buckles me in. I like this. His chuckle disappears as he exits the plane, probably to get the bags from Dimitri. I don't stay awake long enough to find out.

***

"Darce."

I squeeze my eyelids together, not ready to wake. His fingers are soft on my cheek.

"Baby, you can go to the bedroom. We're in the air."

I peek through one lid, finding him staring down at me. "How long have I been sleeping?"

"A half hour. Hard to believe you were passed out the whole ascent…I thought you'd like to sleep in a bed."

"Are you coming with me?"

"I have a video conference, but I'll be in after that."

Unbuckling with difficulty, I stumble over to the other side of the cabin.

The room consists of a queen-sized bed, a dresser, and a loveseat. It doesn't need much else. My luggage is already on the mattress. I reach into it, scavenging for something to wear to sleep. I pick out a pair of shorts and a yellow t-shirt, the first comfortable items I could find. Burrowing myself under the covers, I close my eyes.

However, fifteen minutes later, I'm still blinking, realizing I'm unable to drift off knowing he's outside the room. There's so much I want to ask him about, talk to him about. I sit up, rubbing my face. It dawns on me as I'm yawning that I have no idea where we're even headed.

The room brightens when the door slides open. Benjamin is filling the doorway, surprised to find me awake. "What are you doing up?"

"I wanted to sleep next to you."

"Did you?"

I nod, unfolding the covers on his side. He closes the door behind him quietly, shaking his head.

"I can't. I'm not done."

"What?" I whine.

"You heard me," he hums with a knowing smirk.

"Well, too bad." I grab his tie and pull, eliciting a startled gasp from him as his knee drops forward on the bed. He's laughing when I find his lips. Not one to push me away, he palms the nape of my neck, deepening the kiss with a skilled tongue and determination. Eventually, he begins to ease his way up, something I don't want to allow.

"They're on hold," he reminds me between my desperate assaults. I shake my head, and his mouth curves into a smile against my own. "Darce—"

I groan, letting him go. "All right, okay. Go on."

He's chuckling on his way out. I fall back against the pillows with a huff as he shuts the door. Restlessly, I roll onto my side, then my stomach, until I'm on my back, staring at the ceiling.

Suddenly, the door opens and Benjamin reenters, utterly smug, utterly determined. "I'll call them later."

I sit up onto my elbows. "Yeah?"

He nods, one knee on the bed, reaches out, and curls his fingers into my hair. "Yeah."

***

Surrounded by loud jetting vibrations, which make it near impossible to sleep, I slide my leg around Benjamin's calf while we remain in silence, thousands of feet in the air, headed toward someplace unknown to me. Our skin simmers at our initial touch; our nerves nestled just under in tight, jumbled sections.

They are ignited by a mere graze or caress, and I find contentment in our intimacy. Although it's been weeks since we've rekindled, and months now since I was released from my sentence, he and I have remained firmly in politeness.

We have never been so polite.

Whether we're meeting for dinner or spending the night at one of our apartments, we don't allow arguments. We don't even have to catch ourselves. We talk of everything, everything but what matters.

We haven't spoken of the year apart, what occurred between those months—to the both of us. I wasn't the only person who had to become someone else. Benjamin didn't waste his time alone. He tackled work, his dominating empire, something he had placed on the backburner during the chaos of the trial.

As much as I like politeness, I enjoy truth far better.

"Do you have anything you want to ask me?" I blurt out no louder than a whisper, my cheek burning against his chest. I expect deterring jokes or indifference, or even feigned cluelessness, but Benjamin seems almost armed with an answer, as if he'd had it stored for the right moment.

"Who visited you? Did you make any friends, anyone you could trust there? Was it what you were expecting? The list could go on."

With a pause at the realization that he's been waiting as impatiently as I have, I'm struck with the perfectly unsettling urge to tell him everything, in hopes that barriers will be broken.

"Doris was the only person I allowed to visit."

"Not Kevin?"

"Almost everyone there really liked seeing their family. It makes sense, if you don't think about it too much, to be excited to see your relatives, your friends. That was weird for me. It was hard enough to come out and see Doris, let alone imagine anyone else. In that situation, I liked being alone."

"So, that probably answers my other question."

My eyes rest in the dark on my nails, manicured and crimson red. It's easy to remember when they were broken and surrounded by bruised knuckles.

"I didn't trust anyone. I couldn't there."

"Why not?"

"Because they knew who I was. They knew about the trial, or about you and me. In there, I was famous and privileged in their eyes."

"Didn't you tell them otherwise?"

"That's not how things work in there, Ben."

He scoots off the pillows to meet me eye-level, and I settle my temple into the crook of his shoulder and arm. His hand leaves my hip and drifts along the scar, now a dull pink color beside my ear.

"Is that why this happened?"

"I'm not sure."

His gaze doesn't falter, but those green eyes do soften, holding an unhealthy amount of misplaced guilt. My head shakes just enough for him to sigh and cover my hip again.

"Tell me about you," I whisper, wishing to relieve some of the heaviness that has showed.

"What do you want to know?"

"Everything. Tell me about Dimitri and your family. Tell me about the mergers and crazy contracts."

"You're really interested in hearing about work? Really?"

"I've always enjoyed it, you know that."

"I thought you were pretending because you liked me."

"Is that so?"

He chuckles, offering the widest smile. He's reaching.

"You know, if you hadn't been so stubborn and impulsive, I wouldn't even have to ask you about those mergers. I'd be helping you with them, you know, like when I was your assistant? Before you fired me—"

"Okay, okay, we don't talk of that," he muses, holding me tighter. "Besides, if you were still my assistant, you wouldn't be the up and coming editor you are now."

"True."

He smiles at my lack of modesty, appearing to enjoy it. "Man, it seems so easy to fall back into this…but hard too."

He doesn't have to elaborate. "This" means our relationship which, at the time of the trial, was stronger than steel. We'd conquered the holidays and made it out with a glow that even newlyweds would envy. Over the course of a year apart, the love didn't diminish but became draped in anger and distance. It's both hard…and easy to drop that protective layer.

"I hoped it would have been easier…my way. I never set out to hurt you."

"I know you didn't."

A piece of information he told me in his anger drifts into my brain and holds, so hard I can't help but voice it.

"You told me that you didn't work for a month."

For the first time, his eyes leave mine, settling on my throat. They close when my fingers travel over the sharpness of his jaw onto freshly shaved skin. It feels good to hold him beneath my hand, powerful.

"Everything you're thinking I felt, I did."

"We're together now," I tell him.

"I know," he says and looks at me, finally.

"What made you want to go back?"

"My sister. She showed up, kicked me into shape. My assistant voiced her concerns to Rebecca, who flew over and eased my wounded ego enough to put on a suit and leave the apartment."

"I really like her."

"She's always liked you."

"Even now?"

"Especially now."

"Why?"

"Because only you can evoke those kinds of emotions from me. I'd never been in love…and she knew that."

Despite the countless times he's told me of his love, I'm somehow still caught off guard. For most of our relationship, my love for him was at the forefront of every action between us, every conversation. And after he admitted it, we began to slowly accept the verbalization of it. He makes it look easy now.

"We can get back there, Ben. I know we can. We aren't beyond repair."

"We will get back there. I intend to do everything in my damn power to get us there."

He snakes his arm around my hip, bringing me closer. We both sigh, and I watch his eyes close before I allow mine to do the same.

"Is that what this is all about? This trip?"

"That's exactly what this is about."

I hide my smile. "Where are we going?"

"Bali."

CHAPTER TWO

"Take my hand," Benjamin says as we file out of the airport among many other bright-eyed tourists. The Indonesian air is so thick I can hardly breathe. I take his outstretched hand, knowing if I don't, there will be a very probable possibility I'll lose him on the way out of here.

We're lacking the security we'd usually have following us on a trip of this magnitude, which is worrisome, considering how present he and I have been lately in the news. But Benjamin's made it very clear he intends to have me to himself, with no distractions. Dimitri had to sit this one out.

We approach a short man holding a sign with Benjamin's name on it. "Hello, Mr. Scott. I'm Farel. I will be your chauffeur for the duration of your visit."

"Pleasure, Farel." They shake hands, and Ben gestures to me. "This is my girlfriend, Darcy."

"Welcome to Bali. Right this way. The car is parked just outside. Is this your first trip here?"

"Second for me. First for her."

Like a stupid teenager, I'm stuck on the word girlfriend, pleased to hear him say it to a stranger. The drive to the villa is long and draining, considering the lack of sleep and jet lag, which has descended upon us both. When we finally arrive, Benjamin ushers me from the car with apprehension, waiting for my reaction. Which is stupor. I whip my head from the monstrous resort home to his face in disbelief.

The private villa is entirely encased in crystal clear glass, surrounded by lush green vegetation and tall, straight palm trees. A narrow stone path leads us to the whitewashed French door. He lets me race ahead of him first, obviously savoring my reaction. There seem to be endless rooms. The main living spaces are spacious, teeming with flowers and fresh fruit. Colorful mimosas are laid out on the table for us. My mind implodes at the sight of the plunge pool, which has an entire side of glass dedicated to overlook the ocean, just a few paces of sand away.

"So, good choice?" Benjamin asks warmly, informing me he's been watching me spin in circles.

"This is unreal."

"This is our reality for the next four days. Ultimate seclusion. No one here but you and me." He circles my waist with his arms.

"I like that idea."

"Are you tired? I know the flight was brutal."

"I can survive if you have something you want to do."

"No, get some sleep. Everything will still be here when you wake up." He kisses me, offering a seemingly unending supply of tender care. His gentleness is disarming but appreciated. This trip feels like a force of nature, the remedy to our problems. We've only just arrived, and I'm reassured we're going to come out of this stronger than going in.

I wake a few hours later, not because I'm ready to. My curling stomach has flipped and forced me out of my comatose state. Jet lag has descended, and the only way to get rid of it is a cold shower. Shedding my nightgown, I step into the shower with hopes that the nausea will miraculously disappear. However, within minutes, I'm jumping out of the glass fully drenched, just making the toilet to heave violently into the bowl that reeks of strong bleach. To make sure I'm done, I lay on my knees, my burning cheek against my arm propped on the seat. When it's clear that my stomach has stopped turning, I pick myself up off the puddle I've created and reenter the shower, hoping it doesn't happen again. After brushing my teeth vigorously, I drape on a delicate blue sundress and exit the room, in search of the mogul I'm in love with.

I find him barefoot on the patio in jeans and a white t-shirt, leaning against the railing on the phone, always working. I slide the door open, hit by a wave of boiling heat, and smile when I catch his eye. He holds his arm open, and I walk into him, glowing at this picture.

Benjamin and this backdrop.

"Yes. Yes, tomorrow. No exceptions. Yes. Goodbye." He hangs up, leaving his phone on the laptop set on the wood railing. "You okay?"

"Yeah, just a little sick from the plane, I think.

I'm fine."

"You sure? You want to lie down some more?"

"No, I'm fine, really. What have you been doing?"

"I spoke to a few people, Rebecca included. She told me to say hello to you."

The mention of Benjamin's sister, the only member of his family who can stand me, is welcome. "How is she?"

"Pregnant." He chuckles fondly at my gaping.

"That's so wonderful! How far along is she?"

"Not sure yet."

"I'm so happy for her. That's amazing."

He nods, kissing my forehead. "I had a surprise for you, but I don't know if we should do it now."

"I'm *fine*, Ben. What is it?"

"Come with me." I take his outstretched hand, following him down the beaten path. As we near the water, my feet sink into warm white sand.

A table is isolated under a towering canopy, blocking the scorching sun from the feast on display. The sight is a dream, organized and staged to perfection. I smile widely, squeezing his hand. He raises it, pressing his lips to my knuckles.

***

I sip my second glass of sangria, completely unwilling to take my eyes off the man in across from me.

Benjamin lifts himself up from the seat abruptly. "Aren't you hot?"

With a dizzy grin, I nod. I'm drunk. Stupefied, I

watch as he reaches behind his back and grabs the top of his shirt. The white fabric falls to the sandy floor, and he reaches down and begins unbuttoning his jeans.

"Ben! Someone could see you!" I set my drink down with a thud.

"Private beach, Darcy."

He discards the pants too, leaving him scantily clad in black briefs. I admire his toned body, frozen in my seat.

"You coming?"

He sheds the remainder of his clothes en route to the water. Despite his assurances, I sweep the area thoroughly, searching for other people. Benjamin is unperturbed, waist deep in the water. Mirroring the mixture of colors in the sky, the water is relatively calm and inviting.

I take a deep breath and cross my legs, admiring him from afar as he dives under the waves. He surfaces and raises his arms, smoothing his hair back, knocking the breath from my lungs. Jesus. He's straight out of a Harlequin novel.

Standing, I remove my dress and undergarments on the trek through the mounds of sand, fully aware his eyes are on me. Thankfully, the liquor is making me brave. I stop at the shoreline hesitantly. "Isn't this feeding time? The sharks are going to get us."

He laughs, swimming forward to me. "The only thing that's going to get you is me."

"Is that so?" I giggle as his arms entrap my waist, dragging me to him. "*Oh.*"

He isn't kidding. The proximity of our nakedness and the rushing of the waves shoving us together have made my skin tingle and his body rise to the occasion.

"Yes, *oh.*" He tilts his head up to meet my lips. We connect passionately, his arms keeping me afloat. I wrap myself around his neck, his wet hair soaking my palms.

"I want you," he breathes the moment he breaks away. He shivers beneath my searching caresses before reaching up, fisting my hair in a tight grip. I cling to him as he straightens, walking toward the shoreline with me in his arms.

I've completely lost the unease at the thought of others by the time we're on sand. The air suffocates us between our persistent mouths while he lays me down on the soft, moist sand. With a good idea of how messy this will be, I pull him down on me, giggling when the water hits us, causing us to awkwardly collide.

He shakes his head, chuckling. "This seemed a lot better in my head."

"I like it." I press my lips to his. He drags his fingers over my heaving breasts, and my blushing nipples stiffen against the feather-light touch. He continues further down over my ribs, the dip of my waist. I'm trembling when he passes my pelvic bone, aching for him. He slides two fingers through my clenching apex with intent to relieve. I tangle my hands into his sand-soaked hair.

"I want to feel you inside me," I profess, not interested in foreplay. His eyes sparkle at the confession, digging my own impatience. Obliging me, he spreads me out with the weight of his body and enters me slowly, his mouth gaping in pleasure.

His next thrust triples in strength, forming a familiar rhythm neither of us can resist.

"Fuck, I've missed this," he says darkly, adoring my jaw line.

I cling to him, unaware of water or sand or the setting sun. "I feel so close to you."

He laces our fingers together, digging both our hands into the ground, continuing to plow right through me, determined to propel us to infinity. By the time we slow, trembling around one another, the sun is long gone.

***

Humming, I tilt my head back into Benjamin's skilled fingers. He's been massaging coconut shampoo into my hair for about five minutes now, and I've reveled in every second. I lean my body into his, calm for the first time in weeks…months.

I knew we needed this, but sitting here, without either of our cells disrupting the serenity, I almost lost the aspect of seclusion, of intimacy.

"I'm really happy we're here," I say when he motions for me to rinse.

"This place is amazing."

The shower water washes the suds of fragrant shampoo from my hair. "No. I mean, yes, it is, but I meant us. I'm happy we're here…together."

His eyes swim with warmth when I tilt my cheek into his outstretched hand. "We always will be."

"And you're so sure of this how?" I grab the loofa, squirt a healthy amount of body wash onto it, and drag the small, foamy bundle of material over his shoulders, moving along the curve of his collar bone.

"Because I love you," he says, his voice echoing against the glass. "We always come back to each other, Darce. There's no staying apart. I've come to that realization by now."

His words ignite something deep inside of me, something pushed into a forbidden crevasse. The past year without him, the past month with him…we haven't been the same. Part of me wasn't sure we'd be able to recover what we'd lost in our time apart. When he notices how my eyes are shiny with water that isn't a result of stinging soap, his face etches with concern. I'm more fragile than I've ever been. I thought jail would make me harder, make things seem uncomplicated in comparison, but I'm disoriented. My whole life seems disoriented.

Benjamin gathers me in his arms. "What's wrong?"

"I've been so scared that we…that we wouldn't be able to get past what happened."

He pulls back, taking hold of my face. "You're not going to lose me. You never did, even when you were gone."

An overwhelming rush of solace drapes over me.

You're not going to lose me.

Already surrounded in his grip, I lift myself, circling my legs around his hips.

"Never." I shake my head, my lips to his lips, his cheeks, his forehead, his jaw. "Never."

He plants a steady hand to the wall of the shower, and my back feels the chill of the tile.

His face is buried in my neck, his breath short. "Jesus Christ. Darcy."

We caress each other with longing, our movements searching. His eyes twinkle when our noses, pressed so close, nuzzle, his breath sweet and hot against my lips.

"Marry me."

I freeze against him instantly, positive I heard him wrong. "What?"

He meets my gaze of shock with a serious swallow, and I stop breathing altogether.

"Marry me, Darcy. I…I want to. I want this, more than I've ever wanted anything in my life."

I open my mouth hesitantly. "You want to marry me?"

"Yes."

"Really?" I say, completely disbelieving.

"Say yes," he orders with a nervous smile.

"*Yes!*" I respond, the word slipping through my lips at lightning speed. "Fuck yes."

Blissful by my reply, he crushes his mouth to mine with a low moan, reminding me of his fear of commitment that has miraculously disappeared with those words. I want to be all over him, all at once. We scratch and claw, soaking in the surprise. His hands travel over my flesh, and yet I can hardly feel it. My skin seems unattached to my skeleton, my nerves and veins conjoining together to blow me apart.

"Tomorrow, Darcy," he mumbles into my mouth. "I want to marry you tomorrow, here."

I nod, hardly listening to him. I'd do anything right now.

"*Yes?*" he gasps, eyes wide.

Marry him. Here. Tomorrow.

Even when I force myself to think about it, the answer remains unchanged.

"You don't even want to think on it? I mean, we're eloping…on our own. Do you want that? Are you sure you want this?"

I smile brightly, enamored by his vulnerabilities. "I don't care where or when we do it, Benjamin. I'll marry you anywhere, any day, under any circumstance. Now kiss me."

"God, I love you," he whispers, closing the short space between us. I can't stop smiling even immersed in his kiss, not surprised that my speech has suddenly failed me.

***

The steam clears my skin, the water draining over my body as I stand beneath the nozzle, letting the warmth relax my tense muscles. Last night was sleepless, and for a good part of the morning my eyes remained locked on the ceiling.

I'm getting married. Today.

My inkling is that this trip was premeditated and for this one purpose. Benjamin's phone call on the porch makes complete sense now, when he was demanding for someone to have things ready by today.

He knew I'd say yes. I'm not sure whether to be flattered or embarrassed, wondering how enamored I must be of my love to give him so much assurance. I'm going to marry him today, in some dress I packed and devoid of guests. We've stuck to only one tradition: last night Benjamin slept in a separate room, despite my complaints, not wishing to tempt luck.

I've known this man for nearly two years, and for most of that, his idea of love was a prison sentence, a mistake to all parties. His role models for love were traumatically poor, his mother and father having ruined the concept with their distaste for one another's presence, and Benjamin felt it all. The fact that he even wants to marry me now is a shock. Maybe it's the reason I'm so fearful, now that the initial high has settled, and part of me is expecting him to change his mind.

I try my hardest not to nick myself with the razor as I roughly go over my necessary body parts. My hands won't stop shaking. By the time I'm done grooming, it's been over an hour. I wrap the towel around my body, tucking it into the top to secure it, and walk back into the room.

Lying on the mattress are a clear clothing bag and a floral bouquet.

He didn't…

I unzip the bag, revealing a white wedding dress. I pull it out and hold it up. It drapes to the ground in soft satin, a flowing material that will ripple against the wind off the ocean. I admire the design, the low dip in the back, and my pre-wedding jitters reach an all-time high. I'm reminded that Benjamin dropped this off and is here somewhere, also getting ready, likely overthinking like I am.

Refusing to spend my entire morning in reflection, I apply a shimmer to my eyes and a minimal layer of lipstick, deciding natural is the best way to go. My hair will remain down and, God willing, will not become a knot on the ocean breeze. Standing in only a pair of white lace panties, I stare down at the dress and swallow hard.

Doris is going to kill me.

I slide the dress over my head, letting the material glide over my skin, caressing my curves until it hangs, ending just above my ankles. The straps are delicately thin, the v-cut neckline descending down onto my breasts tastefully. The moment it's on, my mouth feels like cotton. Blood is speeding through my veins.

This is all real.

Distracted by a distant noise from outside the room, and recognizing it instantly, I'm unable to sustain control. The noise is Benjamin, and I can't stay away. Knowing I shouldn't, I peek through the light curtains, needing the glimpse of him.

He's pacing barefoot on the new walkway that has been added for the ceremony, his phone to his ear. He's dressed in cream-colored slacks, a white dress shirt tucked into them that hugs his defined physique. The material of the shirt waves against the wind. His arm sports the watch I gave him, gold and black onyx, and his hair is wild and untamed in the wind, but he isn't focused on it.

"Enrique, stop. A pre-nup isn't happening."

The sentence stuns me, although it shouldn't.

Benjamin shakes his head at whatever Enrique is saying, his hand clenched into a fist at his side.

A pre-nuptial agreement is desired for a man of his standing. He owns most of New York and various other pieces of the world. His fortune must be protected. The only reason my mood shifts at the word is the implication that I'll be marrying him for money.

The thought of a contract being laid out before me, obscene numbers granted to me in case this marriage should fail, as if I wanted any of that from him, ignites a sour taste in my mouth.

"She isn't like that. For heaven's sake, you spent time with her! You know she isn't capable of being that cruel…I know, of course I know money changes people. It's not like that with her."

He listens for a long time, clearly frustrated, dragging his hand through his hair and tugging on the ends. "I don't want to ask that of her. You don't understand. It will ruin everything."

I can imagine Enrique's response. *You have to protect yourself, Benjamin.*

"Fine, send it to me." He hangs up and remains completely still, consumed in his own thoughts while the company sets up the altar by the ocean.

My cheeks are aflame. I'm not sure if it's embarrassment, for him or for me.

While I despise the aspect of it, his lawyer is right. Benjamin has every right to protect himself. I sit on the bed, needing to rid of the unease that has befallen me for eavesdropping on a conversation I should never have heard, and wait to hear his footsteps.

They come only moments later, accompanied by a soft rap on the door.

I stand nervously. "Come in."

Benjamin opens the door, standing under the

threshold, dauntingly beautiful.

"You aren't supposed to see the bride before the wedding."

He's visibly uncomfortable, holding himself stiffly. It's clear he's come to inform me of the prenuptial agreement. "I know. I'm sorry. I just have to talk to you about something before we do this."

"Okay."

I expect him to speak, but his eyes do all the talking, gliding over my face, the dress. His intent is flattering, easily warranting a blush in my cheeks as I wait for him to say something else.

"You're magnificent, Darcy," he admits, no doubt recognizing my hesitance.

"Thank you."

"I'm serious." He steps into the room. "I'm so lucky to have you…lucky you want to marry me."

He comes close enough to take my hand but won't meet my gaze.

"Well, I came in here to, uh, to tell you…" He clears his throat, trying to find the right words, and I give him the time to do it. "To…to see if you wanted to stay a couple of days longer."

That wasn't what I was expecting, and judging by the way his breath leaves him quick, his chest deflating, it wasn't what he was expecting either.

He didn't do it. He didn't ask.

I try to recover as fast as I can. "Stay longer?"

"Yes. We could make this our honeymoon," he continues, nodding mostly to himself. When he lifts his gaze from my hand, his eyes clearing the fog, I realize he's thrown away the idea of asking. I agree with a nod. He caresses the skin between my thumb and forefinger and smiles.

"All right, then."

He turns with the intent to leave.

I'm blurting out words before I even know it. "I'll sign anything you need me to, Ben."

He freezes, his shoulders tensing for a moment. When he twists, his eyes clouded yet again, he recovers his disbelief. "How did you know?"

"I heard you." I gesture my head toward the sliding glass door.

"I'm sorry you heard that. I didn't want to upset you."

"I understand you're an important man, Ben. It's smart for you to do it, so I'll sign whatever you like."

"You're not signing anything except our marriage certificate."

I stare at him.

"I trust you with everything I have. I trust you, and I never want you to believe I don't. I had honestly forgotten about even the possibility of one until he called me after I emailed him about our wedding plans."

"Are you sure? Benjamin—"

"We're not talking about this anymore," he says sternly. Having lost all hesitance he exuded when he entered, he takes me in his arms.

"Let's get married."

My smile widens. "Let's do it."

***

"The Wedding March" is being played by a lone violinist, and the cheerful melody makes my knees knock together in fear. I focus on my bare feet against the makeshift aisle that has been assembled, which is leading me toward the shoreline and toward my future husband.

Conjuring up all courage within me, I lift my gaze, my heart beating wildly. At the end of the aisle, Benjamin is staring at me, a smile splitting his face in two. It's an unusually breathtaking smile, and oddly, one I've never seen before. It's contagious. I can't control mine either.

I'm the luckiest woman alive. I know it full well. If it wouldn't make me a complete fool, I'd be running to him. Benjamin takes my hand the minute I'm close, planting me before the minister, who smiles at both of us.

When he begins to speak, my eyes soak in the setting. The clear sky, the singing wind through the branches of the trees, the crash of waves along the shoreline. Sand swirls in the air but magically doesn't hit us.

It's perfect we're alone. I look back at him, blushing when I find him watching me.

I'm saying "I do" before I know it, holding my breath as I wait for his vow. With relief, I let out that breath as the two words ring strong and confident in his low tone.

There's no dreaded pause of thought, no crack in the declaration.

We're both clearly so sure of this.

When rings are produced, I chuckle, amazed by how much Benjamin was able to accomplish with only a day to prepare. He takes the slim silver band and slips it onto my finger. Visibly shaking, I take his and, less confidently, slide it onto his ring finger. He flexes his hand and admires it, his expression full of wonder.

I doubt he ever believed he'd have such a promise on his hand.

Our eyes don't leave each other as the minister concludes the ceremony.

Benjamin squeezes my hand tightly and mouths, "I love you."

With hopeful tears in my eyes, I mouth it back.

"You may kiss the bride."

We collide, as if we've been waiting our entire lives to make it to this point and can only now race to the finish line. His hands are buried in my hair, my fingers pressed to his smooth jaw. Our mouths, pressed and formed as one, begin to smile together.

When we detach and everything in my world tilts on axis, only then does this become real. Benjamin's lips are against my ring finger, and my eyes are drinking in the sight of him…my husband.

CHAPTER THREE

True to his word, the only contract I signed was the marriage certificate.

Darcy Scott. *Mrs. Benjamin Scott.*

The water paints orange and red in front of me, the Indonesian air thick and moist. Benjamin is escorting the wedding crew to the boat that will allow us to be alone once again. My mind is alive, full of accomplishment and blinding happiness. Because as of today, Benjamin is truly mine.

Having not heard him approach, arms encompass my waist from behind. Knowing it's only him and me, I relax into his hard frame, wanting to remain in this moment for just a bit longer.

The sky is a hazy pink color when Benjamin slips his hand into mine and laces our fingers together. We enter the bedroom, a quiet understanding between us. While Benjamin flicks on a light, I stand at the threshold, hardly breathing, oddly nervous.

"You're my wife," he says, planting himself a few feet from me.

I nod and he chuckles, shaking his head.

"What?"

Obviously amused, he says, "I just never thought I'd ever say that."

He saunters to me, taking his time crossing the space. When my cheek is against his palm, my eyes close, savoring his touch. "I never want you to stop saying it."

"I never will."

Benjamin bends his head, sealing his mouth over mine, ridding the entire world from this room. There is no past, no other life we have to go back to. Right now, we are our own entity, safely trapped in this private place where we can love and scream and worship without reluctance.

Our hands move in patterns. In his caresses, he relieves the straps from my shoulders and, tracing my curves with his palms, urges the soft material down. The dress slides on its own until it passes my hips and drops with finality around my feet. I've worked over his chest, untucked and buttoned his shirt, which displays a glimpse of the washboard abs hidden beneath.

His breath is coming in short gasps when I'm discarding his belt, adoring his chest with rough kisses. His skin tastes of ocean and flames that came from the fire pit that's still roaring outside. Driven mad, I praise him with desire, trailing myself down his body while my hands shove his slacks lower until he can step out of them. My lips hover over the trail of hair at the base of his stomach, my hand stretching over the front of his briefs.

I'm on my knees, consumed by so much need that I can hardly move.

I take hold of his briefs and slowly guide them down, my face tilting up to give him my eyes. His eyes won't miss this, his hand sinking into my hair.

The second I take him in my mouth, his head falls back, a startled sound erupting from his chest. Enjoying his abandon, I watch intensely while he struggles to keep his composure, struggles for air. I trail my fingers over his muscular thighs, and a shudder snakes through him.

My hair is trapped tight in his grip as I lap the length of him, dragging my tongue over his girth. He's extremely aroused, painfully erect due to my teasing.

When I suction my mouth around him, taking as much in as I can, he gives himself into his surrender, allowing me to own him, to completely overpower him. It won't last for long, so I bask in it.

"Fuck," he gasps when my fingers descend further than his cock to massage his balls, intent on running this pleasure through. However, his grip tightens on my hair almost painfully as he drags me back up to his face. "I need you."

He devours my mouth, forcefully enough that I fall back a step, but he catches me. He guides me without breaking toward the bed, until my knees hit the side.

While I scoot back into the mattress, he follows, a dark, sexy presence ready to possess me. My arms surround him as he settles naturally between my legs. His mouth drifts from mine to my jaw, my earlobe, my throat, until he's hovering against my breasts. His fingers knead the peaks, no doubt feeling how fast my blood is pumping, evidence of what he does to me.

He devotes his mouth, his tongue, his attention to my nipples, suckling greedily. His teeth nipping make goose bumps arise throughout my skin. He's ravenous and intense, sliding my panties down my thighs, his breath hot against my ribs.

"I can't believe we're married," I whisper into suffocating air. When he's rid me of my last article of clothing, his hands glide up my legs and flatten against my thighs, spreading them further apart so he can move over me.

"I like it," he responds.

I'm small beneath him and aware of how massive he is. His dark green eyes gleam with lust, urged on by my submission. We're pressed up to each other, hands full of sensitive flesh as he slides into me slowly.

He swallows my moan with his mouth and rocks into me, leaving one hand beside my head to steady himself. I expect his usual aggression but receive something else entirely. Instead of rough torture, mind-blowing pounds, he grinds into my cervix with slow passion. A smile breaks across his face while he looks down at me, and I'm breathless.

He looks so happy.

His body is heavy on mine, but the perfect kind of heavy. It's the heaviness you hope to feel every day for the rest of your life.

Joined in the deepest way possible, I'm struck by realizations, one that stands out above all the others.

I'll never be alone again.

No matter what happens from here on, I know he's with me, and that's enough.

It's really enough.

Somewhere we shift, both ending on our sides, my back molded against his chest. He enters me from behind, wrapping an arm around my shoulders. His hand is burning my hip. His moans praise my ears as he presses his face into my neck, giving all to me.

My muscles tense, contracting as they prepare for a wave of pleasure. He's buried deep, nudging my cervix over and over again. My own shaking rakes through him.

"Ben."

"Come, love. Come for me," he urges, aware of how close I am. At the first explosion, I squeeze my eyes shut, my mouth dropping open as the orgasm courses through me in repetitive droves. Instead of following suit, he continues to slide in and out, dragging on the ecstasy. His lips are at my neck when I come down, but he doesn't let go. He grasps my jaw, snapping it toward his. He takes my mouth fiercely, and his rhythm strengthens.

"Touch yourself," he whispers onto my lips, indicating he's not going to come until I do again. I lay my trembling fingers over my sensitive sex and bite my lip while I circle my clit.

He groans, shoving his head into my shoulder, never faltering. "God, you're clenching so hard around me." He kneads my breast, my puckered nipple. Our bodies coated in sweat, we move in perfect unison, unnaturally aware of each other's bodies.

"I'm going to come," I say, knowing I'm about to scream. He grabs my face, nodding as he kisses me.

"Fuck, baby. Yes, do it," he gasps.

I cry out, unable to stop my body from squirming. Benjamin covers my fingers with his hand, rubbing out the pleasure to make sure I experience my full orgasm. His thrusts begin to slow, his breath catching against my face as he lets go and with one final slam releases himself within me.

Time stops. We lay suspended in the astonishment, the aches, the high, completely still. His chest moves in time with mine, his gulps of air just as desperate as my own. He only shifts to pull me closer, one hand covering my breast as he nuzzles into my throat.

I lean my head back onto his chest. He moves my damp hair away from my face and rests his head on my shoulder.

"That was amazing," I whisper. I feel his body shake with soft laughter.

"Yes, it was."

I can't help shivering as he gently runs his hand over the length of my body. Happily enclosed in this warm embrace, I stare at the silver band on my hand. Reaching down, I take his hand off my breast and hold it up with mine, examining both our rings. Without looking back, I know he is too.

"I can't believe we did this."

"I thought of it before," he admits after a moment. This is news to me.

"When?"

"Just before the trial."

I tilt my head to find his eyes, disbelieving. "The trial? I was a constant mess those months. You wanted to marry me?"

"Yes, although it would have been to prove something, rather than what this was…I wanted you to know I wasn't going to leave."

"I could have been sentenced to a lot more time, Ben. Years, a lifetime. That would have been insane."

He stares at me, blinking slowly. "Darcy, you are it for me. You have to know that by now."

I brighten, finding it hard to remain still.

"I couldn't have this with anyone else. I wouldn't."

"You are it for me too," I tell him, my heart bursting.

***

We move in unison with each other, reheating the pasta we abandoned in our desperation. I chop the lettuce for the salad while Benjamin sets up the table outside on the patio. Dressed in a matching robe, he looks thoroughly fucked, his raven hair wild in the wind. He heads back into the room, smiling when he catches my eyes on him.

"You better be careful. If you keep staring, you're gonna take off a finger."

I blush what I am sure is beet red. "You, sir, are no gentleman."

He circles the island, sneaking up behind me, and wraps his hands around my waist, kissing the back of my head. “I like you staring at me. God knows I do it enough with you.”

I scoff and roll my eyes but love his words.

“What? You know I can’t stop looking at you.” He moves his hands up to the sash that’s holding my robe together. I stop chopping as he begins to unravel it, reaching one hand under the fabric to grasp my breast. “I can’t keep my hands off of you either.”

The robe parts, and the sash drops to the ground. Nibbling on the sensitive skin below my ear, his other hand travels down…down…*down.*

***

Thirty minutes later, with two more orgasms under my belt, we finally get to the table, ready to eat. Famished but still high from the post-coital bliss, we sit close to each other, eating slow and talking fast.

I lay my legs over his, taking a sip of my wine. “When you said stay longer, did you mean it?”

“Yes. When I talked to Cindy, I told her I was planning to propose and, if possible, elope. Mind you, I wasn’t expecting to do it in the shower, but it just happened. That’s why she let you go at such a busy time. She said to just let her know when you’ll be back.”

“She’s honestly way too good to me.”

I admit, part of me believes she said yes because the publicity will explode upon the news of Benjamin’s nuptials, which will only help her company. But I try to believe she’s truly, genuinely happy for me.

"She admires you. When she told me she was planning on making you an editor, she gushed for a good half hour, not even kidding."

"You talked to her before she did it?" I ask, glancing up at him.

"She called me about two weeks before you were released."

I smile softly, and he raises a brow.

"What?"

"I just…I like knowing that while I was in there, you were thinking about me."

His eyebrows furrow together, and he opens his arms, gesturing me over. I stand from my seat and settle myself onto his lap, surprised at how comfortable he is. I mold into his chest, my knees against his abs. He pulls me close. "Of course I did, Darcy."

"You were so mad at me." I remember the fights that seemed to never end.

"I was. Doesn't mean I didn't think of you."

I close my eyes, listening to the soft thump of his heartbeat. There's suddenly a remote in Benjamin's hand and music, the full crooning of none other than Frank Sinatra.

"Dance with me."

I slide off of him and rise, taking his hand. He walks me to the terrace, the ocean a splendid backdrop behind us. He tugs me close, lacing our fingers together by his chest.

The song is a slow ballad, an emotional testament to true love.

Benjamin's tenderness, his grazing lips against

my knuckles, has been consistent since we arrived. The storm of the past year of our lives has finally passed, and here we are, devoted in the highest possible way to one another.

"I love this song," I say quietly.

"“Night and Day." It's one of my favorites. I thought it was a fitting song for us."

"It's perfect."

We dance our first dance, with no one but each other to know.

***

Our trip passes in a blink of an eye. Trips to exotic towns, scuba diving, hikes, fancy dinners, days completely consumed in sun. Benjamin's like a machine, determined to fill each day with an experience I've never had. When we're not out, we're on the grounds of the villa, rarely ever clothed. The fun seems as if it will never end, that we'll be able to make our own strange life here in this place, and yet the sunsets descend rapidly until there's only one day left to soak all of this up. It all rushes to me while I'm packing.

"The car will be here at seven a.m.," Benjamin announces, entering the room with our bathing suits that dried overnight.

Oddly enough, my eyes are tearing up, my chest inflated with reluctance. Benjamin, a mind reader, wraps an arm around my shoulder from behind, urging me into him. I bite my trembling lip as he kisses my cheek.

What the hell is wrong with me?

He reaches out and stops me from packing with a gentle hand. “What’s going on?”

I shake my head, unable to speak.

“Why are you crying? What happened?”

“I’m being stupid.”

“Something’s obviously upset you.”

“No, that’s what’s stupid. It’s the opposite.” I roll my eyes at my fluctuating emotions.

“You’re crying because you’re happy?”

“I don’t know why I’ve been so emotional lately.” I sniffle when he wipes the tears away.

“Look,” he says, his green eyes alight with admiration, “we had a perfect week, and I’m sure we’ll have many more of them together. We can do this as many times as you’d like. Nothing has to change,” he promises. “We can be this happy.”

***

Lounging in a hammock, experiencing the true definition of being lost in relaxation, Benjamin listens while I read out a selected chapter of a manuscript to him, torn between asking for a full request and passing.

“It’s a bit morbid,” he says when I finish. “I mean, the entire family is terrible to each other.”

“The synopsis says that the brother kills his sister in the end, but it’s a twist.”

“Damn. And I thought my family had set the bar on dysfunctional households.”

I set the iPad aside, enjoying the way his fingers dig into the base of my foot, massaging deeply. I fall silent, in a tranquil state.

"I wish I had the type of family that could be a family to you."

I'm shocked by the admission. His family, apart from his sister, hasn't welcomed me into their lives, and I doubt that will change when Benjamin announces his elopement to them.

"You're the only family I need…you and the family we make together."

"You'd like children?"

I nod, feeling the exact moment this conversation deepens. It's odd this subject has never come up before. "Eventually, sure. It would be nice. Have you ever thought about kids?"

He's noticeably quiet, and it dawns on me that I already know his answer. Benjamin hardly has time for me. He's juggling this whole other world I'm barely apart of and then enters mine, devoting the rest of his time to us.

"I never thought of it. My job takes so much time," he says, confirming my suspicion. "I wouldn't want to bring a kid into this world and treat him the way my father did with me. I would want him to know me."

I understand that. We both have jobs now that take up a lot of time.

He holds me close. "Right now, you're all I need."

***

The initial screech of the alarm on the night table jolts me out of sleep. I flinch and peel my cheek off of Benjamin's chest. He raises his arm off my back and reaches over to silence it.

"What time is it?" I roll onto my pillow that hasn't been touched all night.

He drags a hand over his face. "Five."

"It's too early."

"The car is picking us up at seven, and I was hoping to get a swim in before that."

I don't remember falling asleep again, but when I resurface, blinded by a sliver of light pouring through the closed curtains, Ben is gone. It's 5:30, which means he's probably out in the water. After a quick brush of my teeth, I step onto the terrace in my bikini, searching for a sign of movement in the ocean.

The sun is already rising, halfway to its usual place in the sky. I finally spot him a ways down the beach, his long arms slicing through the current, and set off toward the beach. I'm up to my calves in sea water when he spots me. He smiles and pushes his hair from his face, slicking it back in shiny waves. The black swim trunks are plastered on his muscular thighs, conforming to his masculine shape.

"You look exhausted," he says when he reaches me.

"You don't," I quip suggestively.

His brows soar with pleasure at the compliment. "Come in."

"I'm thinking about it."

"Thinking about it?" He grips my waist.

I glower at him. "You wouldn't…"

"I actually would." He adjusts his grip on my skin with a squeeze. With an inhale, I make a run for it, laughing wildly when he catches me within seconds. He easily heaves me into the air and over his shoulder, resisting my struggling as he directs us toward deeper water.

"Ben, put me down!"

"What was that? I can't hear you!"

Waist deep now, he grabs my hips and lets me slide down his torso, holding me close. I'm desperately trying to maintain a disapproving scowl, but my glee surpasses the attempt.

"All right, I'm sorry," he surrenders, tracing my face with his finger.

I squeal when he catapults me into the air and I drop, sinking into the salty ocean. Sputtering, I reemerge with vengeance. Laughing, he begins to hastily make his way out of the water.

"Oh no, you don't!" I growl, and like a monkey, I latch myself onto his back.

"All right, all right. I give up!"

"You should have thought of that before."

Plowing through the shoreline, he sets me down on the damp sand and makes a run for it. I follow him, determined to reach him. Then he freezes mid-run and pivots, catching me when I launch myself at him.

His kiss is rough, his tongue driving through my lips with crazed madness. I grasp his cheeks between my hands, meeting him with the same amount of breathless passion.

"I'm going to miss this," he says against my mouth.

Me too.

***

The clouds disappear on our descent, New York showing itself in all its majestic glory. There isn't much that can challenge the aerial view of the city in unique beauty. After so long in flight, the ground should be very inviting. And if this were just a normal getaway that led to nothing consequential, going back to our lives wouldn't be so life-altering.

But today, when we land, we will be very different from the people who boarded this jet.

We're married. No one knows. Not my friends, not the press. And we mustn't let the big bad city destroy us. In our very complicated past, our surroundings have been against us. Our jobs, our inner circle, the press…we've been the losing side for so long. A year ago, I was in prison. If there's bad luck, it usually finds me.

This trip was the break I've been waiting for all my life, the piece of the puzzle that makes all the failed tries worth it. Benjamin is mine, for better, for worse, forever.

I fondle the wedding band on my finger absentmindedly while my head swarms with thoughts. The past week has been a dream, a dream where Benjamin is solely focused on our new marriage, on his bride. There were no dwellings on work or family problems or conference calls. Benjamin enjoyed himself, talking and laughing until he was blue.

To know that he will not be able to be that here isn't negative thinking; it's reality.

I fell in love with a business mogul, awed by his

ability to grow. I'd never ask him to abandon that in any way. Loving Benjamin means loving the entire package.

His hand covers mine in my lap, his platinum band shining in the sunlight reflected from the window. "It will be fine, Darce."

"What will?"

"Everything."

He knows me well. I nod, leaning into him.

"I have something to give you." Dressed in a dark chestnut-colored suit, he's the spitting image of the businessman I met nearly two years ago.

"What?"

He releases my hand and digs into his travel bag. The small blue box he takes from it is a staple, a giveaway for lovers. Benjamin's holding a ring, and despite having married him already, my chest expands.

"Ben…"

"Don't say I didn't have to." He smiles, opening it.

"It's true. I already have a ring."

"Not an engagement ring." He lifts an oval-shaped diamond ring from the cloth. The band is a slim circle of silver, delicate and bright. The diamond is flawless, and knowing Benjamin, he'd have inspected it thoroughly before purchasing. "If you don't like it…"

"It's almost too beautiful," I say, awed. "How could I not love it?"

He slides the ring onto my finger, nestling it with my wedding band, then he kisses me, using up the remaining time we have left of our vacation smartly.

CHAPTER FOUR

We brave the airport, bombarded by reporters that have been set on us like hounds from the moment the door to the tarmac opened. My eyes are blind from the flashes of cameras, my hand clutched in Benjamin's hand, which hasn't loosened even the slightest since we encountered our first round of paparazzi. Dimitri met us outside the plane, having already spoken to Benjamin about the impromptu marriage on the phone. His services were desired today.

"Is that an engagement ring? Mr. Scott! Miss Fontaine!"

"No, there are two rings there!"

"Did you elope? A secret wedding?"

"Mr. Scott!"

***

Benjamin and I drop our bags onto the floor of my apartment.

"I don't understand why he can't just come

here?" Benjamin complains.

He didn't take the news of me staying with Kevin tonight too well.

"He's having problems with Doug, and I promised him before we ran out and got hitched."

"You *are* coming to live with me, right?"

"Of course I am. This is only tonight. I'm going to be warm in your bed for many, many nights to come." I kiss his lips lightly. His features begrudgingly smooth, his demeanor lightening at my clarification.

"Nights? I think you mean years, Mrs. Scott."

"I like the sound of that," I giggle, wrapping my arms around his neck. "He won't be here for an hour, you know…" I begin to hint, but Benjamin's one step ahead of me—and drags me further into the apartment.

***

"I've heard this place is good!" Kevin bellows over the roaring music we can already hear from the cab. Still unsure how to confess the past week's events to him, I've hidden my hand from him the entire way here. He's extremely bubbly tonight, which makes me wonder how messed up he really is. The line to the club is long and extends the entire length of the building.

As we walk to the end of the line, it dawns on me that I should have found a time to inform him of my new title in the cab. Nearly everyone in line watches us move, intrigued and probably wondering when my beau will make an appearance.

I shouldn't be surprised when the woman in front of us spins to face us. "Are you Darcy?"

I bob my head uncomfortably. "Yeah."

"Could I get a picture with you?"

"A picture? With me?"

"Yes."

"Um, okay. I've never been asked that before."

She hands over her phone to her friends and stands beside me. The years of avoiding cameras do me no favors. I can barely muster a smile, loathing the thought that this may become a reoccurring thing. Benjamin's the famous one. He has to put up with this stuff. Not me.

"Mrs. Scott?"

I look up from the person taking the picture to see a man in a suit standing a few feet away. "You and your friends may come with me."

With one look at Kevin, I witness the moment he goes from utter confusion to speech-rendering shock. Blushing, I tell the girls they can come with us, following the bouncer with my mute friend. When we're past the rope, Kevin snatches my hand, lifting it into the light.

"Holy fuck!" he gasps upon seeing the large rock on my fourth finger.

"I didn't know how to tell you," I say, blushing wildly as I pull my arm back to my side.

"Please, Mrs. Scott, if you need anything, ask me personally. I would be happy to help you," the bouncer says. He unclips the rope to the VIP lounge, and I redden even further.

"Thank you very much."

We take the stairs to the balcony, losing the

madness of the first floor. There are suits as far as the eye can see. Tables and loveseats fill the room, a bar along the wall stocked with every liquor imaginable. The lighting is dimmed, but that doesn't stop most of the men in the room from locating the group of girls who just entered with Kevin and me.

"Is this all right?" I whisper to Kevin. "We don't have to stay up here if you don't want to."

"This is the VIP lounge, babe. I'm more than happy here." His eyes catch my ring again. "But I need a damn drink."

With a quick goodbye, we depart from the girls and make our way to the bar. Taking a seat, I prepare for a lecture. Kevin orders us two rounds of shots, and the order makes my eyes bug out of my head.

"So we're going there tonight?" I joke, crossing my legs.

"Tell me something, Darcy. Is that an engagement ring that just happened to have two bands to it? Or is that what I think it is?"

"I'm married," I confess, ripping off the Band-Aid. "We eloped in Bali."

He gapes. "I told you to see each other more. That didn't mean run away and get married with no one but yourselves to attend! Doris is going to lose her damn mind."

"He asked me, and I didn't want to wait either. Kevin, it was everything I ever imagined. He was perfect…it was perfect."

"You've been back a few months, Darcy, and nothing felt right, didn't you say that? You and

Benjamin were finding it hard to reconnect?"

"We found our rhythm there. Kev, we were separated against our will. He was angry with me, and I was ashamed by everything that happened, but the love was never not there."

He squeezes my hand. "Don't get me wrong, babe. I'm overjoyed he put a ring on it, but I'm worried you jumped too fast."

"We didn't, Kev. I know we didn't."

A classic Kevin move, he realizes his next words may possibly offend and decides a different course of action…handing me the first shot the bartender offers. And like me, I fumble trying to detour the subject from me. The moment my throat is coated in liquor, the delightful burn sizzling my esophagus, I attempt the segue.

"How about you tell me what's going on with you and Doug?"

"Nothing's going on with me and Doug. That's the problem."

"Did you break up?"

"No, no. We're still together. We're just having problems."

"Such as?"

He leans in, taking my hand. "We haven't slept together."

"Wait, what?"

"Exactly." He leans back in his chair while I snap my jaw shut.

"It's been…over a year, Kev. What's the wait for?"

"Marriage," he says, with a stern glower. Rendered speechless, I blink blankly. While waiting until marriage proves to be a beautiful sentiment, Kevin's not one for abstinence. It's tough to imagine how he's gotten this far without straying, which only shows how much Doug actually means to him.

"Are you going to marry him? I mean, if you've waited this long, it must be for that reason, right?"

"I don't want to get married," he says with a shrug. "Ever."

"Does he know that?"

"Yes. And somehow, we both still keep calling each other at the end of the day. It's like this dead-end road that will lead us over a damn cliff, and yet we make the turn. It's ridiculous. Some days I'm pissed at him, and some days I don't care."

"You love him," I murmur, studying his reaction. I've seen that dead end many, many times and have managed to back up and avoid the cliff. The look I see on his face tells me he'll do the same.

"*Darcy Fontaine.*"

My spine stiffens at the outburst behind me and the voice that I recognize all too easily. With a twist in my stool, I brace myself for unpleasantness.

"Alexander."

My husband's brother is regarding me closely, a feigned sentiment of awe plastered on his face. He fits in with the room, clad in a stiff suit with a suitcase tucked under his arm, as if there were top-secret instructions inside.

"I thought it was you. The tan suits you."

I manage a smile and glance over at Kevin. "Kevin, this is Alexander, Benjamin's brother."

Finishing off his second shot, Kevin says, "Hi."

Alexander smiles enough for it to be passable. "I heard about the trial. Sorry I wasn't there to support you."

My annoyance is irresistible. "You don't like me, Alex. Why would you support me?"

Kevin's a poor bystander, stuck in the thick tension simmering between us.

"Still only have eyes for my brother?"

"You haven't heard? They got married over the weekend," Kevin proclaims, acting as though he weren't just informed of the news himself.

Alexander laughs it off, finding the statement a jest. "No, Benjamin wouldn't marry anyone."

I lift my hand, showcasing my fingers and, more importantly, the rings adorning my ring finger. "It seems he would."

He stares at the rings for a moment, then his lips purse in what looks like anger. "Well, it seems I'm mistaken. Can't blame him, though. You have a way of getting under the skin. I know that firsthand."

Realizing he's referring to the short period of time where he imagined he and I would become something greater, and clearly still hung up on it, I shut it down. "Are you just getting here?"

"No, I actually have to get going." He gestures to a group of men near the door waiting on him. "Give my brother my congratulations. We have to all get together sometime, celebrate this wonderful occasion."

The sarcasm laced in the last part of his farewell isn't lost on me.

"Good to meet you, Kevin. Enjoy."

He walks away stiff as a board, and Kevin chuckles.

"Well, he's definitely not happy you're married."

I glare at him, signaling the bartender. "Another, please."

Kevin whistles, enjoying my sudden delve into liquor.

"I don't understand what that was in the slightest. He loathed me last time we saw each other."

"Wasn't the last time you talked when he confronted you about Benjamin?"

"Yes."

"Seems lover boy was hoping you'd say you'd sworn off the handsome billionaire for good."

As if his ears were ringing, Benjamin's name lights up my phone screen settled on my lap. Kevin and I look dubiously at each other before I stand up and walk toward the bathroom, one hand pressed to my ear to hear better.

"Hi."

"Baby…how are you?"

"Buzzed with no end in sight," I reply.

"I'm not even going to let myself worry about that."

"Right, because I'm more than capable of taking care of myself."

"I know that a little too well," he says warmly. *"But, you know, if you can't find a taxi, just call me and—"*

"Ben."

I hear his smile.

His chuckle makes me wish I were with him.

"Where are you?"

"My office."

"At work? It's nearing midnight."

"I'm catching up. Quite a bit has happened since I ditched my life to marry the beautiful editor with great legs."

"You don't say? Well, this girl is lucky you were so kind as to do that for her."

"I think so." I imagine his smirk, and it immediately brings one to my face. *"You sure you don't want to come crash with me? I could make it worth your while."*

"I have one last night of freedom, hot shot," I respond and lean into the wallpaper. "Kevin will probably stay at my place. I'll see you tomorrow?"

"I'll be there at two."

"It's so sweet you're going to help me pack up my place."

"The sooner you are moved in, the better. I don't sleep well when you're not there."

I try to temper the rising blush in my cheeks with a hand, sure it's useless. I'm dizzy in love and unable to hide it. "Is it bad that I like that?"

"Yes."

I bite my lip, glancing back into the room where Kevin is focused on scrolling through his phone. "I should be getting back to Kevin."

My run-in with Alexander, Benjamin's older, adoptive brother, hovers in my thoughts, reminding me that in marriage, secrets are lethal and destructive. But instead of telling him, knowing I'd ruin his night, I say goodnight without divulging the details.

I'll tell him tomorrow when he can look into my eyes and find it impossible to jump to conclusions.

***

"Tell me how it happened," Kevin asks while we remove the decorative pillows to my bed. We stumbled into the apartment just after one and spent another hour trying to dig through my fridge.

"What?"

He sits on the edge of the mattress, in only his jeans. He has no qualms in being bare-chested in front of me nor tucking himself under my covers either.

"The proposal, the ceremony. I want details."

I bite the inner corner of my lip, pushing my hair to the side. "Uh, well, he actually proposed in the shower."

His smirk extends boldly. "Together?"

I evade his question and go on. "It wasn't like that. It was romantic…I had never expected him to ever propose, let alone demand we do it the next day."

"Only he could get away with something like that. Did you even want to get married?"

"To him, yes."

"You never dreamed of a large wedding with family, friends to surround you? I thought all girls did."

"I never thought there would be a day where I could imagine getting close enough to someone that I'd want to marry them. We married on the beach, with three people watching, and it was perfect,

Kev."

"I'm trying to not get offended. You didn't miss having us there?"

I roll back the comforter, shooting him a glance. "Of course I did. It's just Benjamin and I are different people when we're alone. It's easier…he did mention a celebratory dinner, though."

That perks him up. "Count me in."

"Will I be including Doug on the invite list?"

His smile goes lopsided with defeat. "I'm going to talk to him tomorrow, I think."

"I think you should. He's crazy about you. You can tell when he looks at you."

"I'm going to have to take some pointers from you, married woman. Maybe you'll pass along some luck."

I fall back into the bedding at the same time he does, sinking into the airy gel.

After a life of luck or fate or whatever it can be called against me, his words strike a chord in me. Luck does seem to be on my side, and I can only pray it remains this way.

***

The next morning, Kevin's leaving just as Benjamin's arriving. My husband is scaling the steps fluidly in a t-shirt and jeans, ready to work.

Kevin chuckles when he reaches the top. "Well, well, well…"

My heart flutters as a small, surprisingly shy smile appears on Benjamin's face.

"Hello, Kevin."

"You know, when I said get your ass over here and make up, I didn't necessarily mean marry her right away."

"I decided to skip a couple of steps," Benjamin says, slinging his arm around my back. "Hi, baby."

"Hello," I breathe, bursting at the seams. Kevin rolls his eyes while observing us in our newfound marital bliss.

"Okay, I'm leaving before you two jump each other in front of me."

He doesn't see my gape as he descends the flights. Ben is smiling wide next to me, chuckling softly. Yes, Kevin is a piece of work.

"I don't know why you're laughing!" I exclaim, pinching his abdomen, and even though there's no excess skin to grab ahold of, he shrinks away from me.

"You've gotta admit, he knows us well."

"Oh, does he? Well, not today. We're working. We have my apartment to pack."

He cages me to him, refusing to let me enter my premises. "You own books and a few pieces of furniture. We have plenty time."

"I take offense to that. My apartment is very beautiful and well furnished."

"Your old apartment. You live with *me* now."

"Keep insulting my apartment," I warn, squirming out of his grasp with a coy smile. "See what happens."

He catches me mid-step underneath the entrance, burrowing his face in my hair as I lead him inside.

***

"It's unhealthy how many damn books you have."

"You'd expect less from a bibliophile?"

Ben puts the moving van into park and climbs out with me. We're hidden in the private garage, concealed from press…for now. Memories of the swarms of reporters the day of my bail release reminds me that we're not safe in here. Dimitri and two other men are already waiting, all three of them dressed in casual clothing to help us.

"I have something to show you," Benjamin says, laying a gentle hand on my back, moving me toward the elevator. "Dimitri, I've labeled the ones we're keeping. Everything else goes in storage."

"Got it, sir," Dimitri answers, passing by us. My head swivels around, following them.

"We're not unloading the car with them?"

He chuckles, gesturing me into the elevator. "I pay them to do it, Darce."

A twinge of guilt supersedes my aching bones, mostly because it's my things they have to spend the day storing.

"That reminds me, we need to talk about something," he adds, inputting the penthouse code.

"What?"

"I'm aware we decided not to sign a pre-nup. We do need to talk about money, though."

The bell dings, indicating we've reached our destination. The word is sitting on my tongue, saturating my mouth with distaste. "Money?"

"I plan to buy you a vehicle this week, as well as deposit funds into your account. I wanted to let you know before I did it."

The time ticks by us in silence while we stand in his foyer, a few feet apart from each other.

"What on Earth are you talking about?" I finally ask.

He tilts onto his hip, crossing his arms over his chest. "You knew this was going to happen, Darcy."

"I don't want your money, Ben."

He's expecting a fight, but oddly enough, he seems pleased to hear me say that. And that infuriates me.

"Did you actually think I wanted that? That I want you to support me? I'm not these women you're used to banging."

His eyes narrow at the low blow, which I refuse to take back. "I want to do this, Darcy. You're my wife. I want you to have good things."

"I do."

"Then don't touch it. Don't drive the damn car, but I'm getting it for you."

"So you have final say, huh?"

"Darcy—"

"No, this is my life. If I wanted a car, I'd get one. I make enough money in my job. I don't need yours. I'm not with you for that. You have to know that by now."

"I do know that. I married you because you were different than anyone else. It's *because* you are different that I want you to have it."

I'm shaking with frustration. "Please, Ben. If I need something, I'll ask."

"This is marriage, Darcy! From what I've heard of it, this…this is what normal couples do. They share their possessions with each other!"

"Yeah, they do! But I don't have anything to give you! This is completely one-sided!"

He falls silent at my outburst, and all traction to the argument dissipates upon my candor. Features smooth and eyes searching, he plants himself in front of me and cups my face. "You've given me everything, Darcy. Everything I could have ever wanted. Can't you see that?"

My knees shake weakly.

"On that beach, you gave me happiness, and love, and family, real family. My money is nothing. A car is *nothing*. Let me do it, please. I want to repay you."

My hand flattens on his chest as my breath hitches. "Benjamin—"

"Please, Darcy."

I don't answer him verbally, but I remain silent enough that he understands I'm conceding. He traces the sharp edges of my profile with his thumb gently. "Thank you," he says softly.

"I need a shower."

Reluctantly, he moves to the side and lets me pass, and I leave him so he can revel in his victory. I strip and step into the shower, grimy in more ways than one. The subject of Benjamin's unlimited flow of cash is never a subject I like to dwell on long and one I thought we'd left behind along with the pre-nup conversation.

There's no reason for me to need the money, except to quell his masculinity. I'm living under his roof; everywhere we go he insists on paying. This money he's providing me is solely for lavish reward, and it, like the pre-nup, makes me wonder in the back of my mind whether he truly believes me or is still waiting for the day where I'll prove him wrong and finally max out his account.

I simmer in the thoughts for far too long, making it impossible to calm down by the time I exit the bathroom in a towel. Benjamin is already showered and dressing into one of his usual expensive suits. We lock eyes in the mirror, but not for long.

"Going somewhere?" I ask, sifting through my clothes.

"I have to go into work for a bit."

I'm pulling on a bra when he garners enough courage to approach me, holding a tie. "Would you do this?"

He knows full well how to do a tie, which makes his question one I can't refuse, knowing he's trying to dial down the tension before he leaves.

I hang the sleek fabric around his neck, feeling his eyes on my face as I tuck the fold through the small slot.

"I didn't get to show you the surprise."

"That wasn't the surprise?" I blanch at saying that aloud. "I'm sorry. What is it?"

He turns to the dresser, picking up a black portfolio.

"I know you don't like pictures, but I thought you'd like this."

"I have nothing to hide from anymore. I'll learn to like them." I open the folder and remove the contents inside, finding photographs.

Pictures from our wedding.

"There was a photographer?" I ask in confusion, unable to recall any cameras in sight.

"There was."

"I can't believe I didn't see them."

He smiles, taking the pile. He sifts through them, searching for a specific one. He pulls one out and hands it to me. Tears well up in my eyes at the captured moment of "You may kiss the bride."

We're both struggling to remain serious in our deliriousness in the shot, making us look all the more happy. The kiss is strong, our grip on each other even stronger.

"I can't believe you did this," I whisper.

He smiles, moving a strand of hair from my eyes. "I'm glad you like it."

"Can we put one up?"

"You can put up whatever you want to. This is your house too now."

Somehow, he's rid the tension in mere minutes and replaced it with adoration.

Overwhelming adoration.

***

Doris gives me a curious once-over while I squirm in her island bench, preparing to unload my news that will either make her incredibly happy or incredibly disappointed. Setting the empty tea kettle into her sink, she offers me a mug of earl grey tea.

"So, tell me. How have you been? How are you and Benjamin?"

I'd been hoping Kevin would have spilled the news, but unfortunately, no such luck.

"Married."

As if her face hadn't been disbelieving enough,

the sight of my rings nearly sends her to the floor. "You're *married*?"

"He proposed in Bali and insisted on doing the ceremony there."

She blinks in shock, hands on her hips now. "I never thought he would want to do that. He's always been so against the idea of marriage, considering the severing relationship of his parents. Honey, this was a big step for him, for you both."

"I know it was. We've been doing great, better than great. Although we had an argument about money today."

"Pre-nup?"

"There wasn't a pre-nup."

Her eyes are bugged, but she won't insult me by verbalizing her awe. "Wow, I'm surprised."

"As was I."

"He trusts you."

"He wants to give me money and a damn car. It's ridiculous."

"You don't want him to support you?"

"He already is. All of this other stuff is just taking it over the top. I like working. After so long struggling, I like providing for myself, and he knows that."

"What did he say when you said that?"

"He fought me until I agreed."

"That sounds like him." She rounds the island and takes the seat beside me. "Listen, just let him do it. It's going to make him happy. He's worked hard for his wealth, and he's never had someone to pamper before."

"How am I supposed to take these things from

him like it's a normal thing?"

Doris shrugs. She doesn't know either.

***

I'm stirring creamy Alfredo sauce into a serving bowl full of al dente pasta, ravenous from the smell of garlic and heavy cream filling the apartment. The table is set, despite the unknown whereabouts of my partner. I'm slicing a loaf of bread when Benjamin makes his appearance, accompanied by the ding of the elevator.

"It smells good in here," he says, setting his briefcase on the table. He's in a far better mood than when we parted, and so am I. Doris helped, as usual.

"Chicken Alfredo. Sit down. I'm almost done."

I tilt my cheek into his lips as he molds to my back, laying his hand over mine with the knife. "Let me serve you."

"I'm really almost done."

"Just sit down," he presses, kissing my shoulder. I do as asked while he loads our plates.

"I talked to my sister about us," he says, slathering a piece of bread with a thin coating of butter. The mention of her reminds me of my run-in with his brother, which I have forgotten until now.

"What did she say?"

"She's ecstatic about the proposal, pissed as hell about the wedding."

"I figured as much," I say, noticeably uncomfortable as I gear for an unpleasant conversation. "I forgot to tell you…I ran into your brother last night."

His movements slow while he places my plate in front of me. "My brother?"

"Yes, when I went out with Kevin."

Clearly ticked off, he takes the seat next to mine. "Did you tell him about us?"

"Of course I did."

"I'm guessing he didn't take it well."

"He acted odd and uncomfortable, strangely enough."

"It's not odd he found you marrying someone else displeasing."

His eyes narrow at my eye roll.

"Well, what did he say?"

"He said congratulations and that we should have a dinner to celebrate with your family, although I'm not really sure if he was being condescending."

He stands and enters the kitchen, retrieving a wine glass. "Want a glass?"

"No thank you."

"I'm not subjecting you to that," he says, lowering back down into his seat.

"Last time wasn't *that* bad, Ben."

"My father insulting you in every way possible wasn't bad enough?"

"I think we should try it again before we completely write them off forever. I mean, they *are* your family."

"And you know how I feel about them."

"I do. And if you really don't want to do it, then we don't have to. But I figured they'd like to find out about us from something other than a TV or newspaper."

He nods, probably just to placate me.

***

Catapulted out of sleep by a violent twisting of my insides, I scramble out of bed, the way to the bathroom illuminated by the sun that's still rising outside the windows. My knees buckle, aching from the force of my fall so my face can reach the toilet in time. With only seconds to dread what's coming, the tightening in my esophagus comes, and I'm vomiting.

The painful heaves last under a minute, having taken all my energy. I lay my hand on my arm, waiting to see if it really is over.

Food poisoning is my initial thought, but since Benjamin is fine, that seems unlikely. My eyes open and close tiredly, my mind trying to shut down, not ready to wake fully. Refusing to fall asleep here, I dig through my unpacked box of toiletries for my toothbrush.

The sight of an unopened box of tampons stuns me, and my digging stops.

The sight of them reminds me of how long it's been since I used one.

My heart plummets, horror rendering me immobile.

No, it can't be. It can't.

"Darcy?"

My husband appears in the doorway, shirtless, right out of sleep.

My voice comes out an octave higher than it should when I answer. "What?"

"You okay?"

I nod, taking my toothbrush from the pile and stuff the box back under the counter. "Yeah, yeah. I'm fine. Had a nightmare."

He comes up behind me, kisses my hair, and begins stripping out of his clothes for a shower. "Shower with me."

Panicking more than he could ever know, I inch away from him, forcing a smile. "I have to make a call first."

I race out of the room, toothbrush still in hand, before he can suspect anything.

My bag nearly falls out of my hands as I fish around for my cell phone. When I do find it, I dial my gynecologist I last saw months ago when prescribing my birth control.

"Dr. Trigiani's office. How may I help you today?"

"Hi, I know this is last minute, but I was wondering if I could possibly schedule an appointment with the doctor today."

"She had a cancelation. I could fit you in at noon. Does that work for you?"

I press my hand to my thumping chest. "Yes."

"Just a check-up visit?"

"Um, yes. A check-up."

"Absolutely. And your name?"

After giving her everything necessary, I hang up and drop the phone and my bag onto the bed, dizzy from the speed at which my brain is working. It's not what I think it is…it can't be.

***

"Darcy."

I glance up from the newspaper. Benjamin has finished his breakfast and looks as though he's been watching me for a while.

"What?"

"Are you all right?"

"I'm fine."

"You sure? You've been reading that same paragraph for twenty minutes now."

I stand up and start clearing the table. "Yeah, I'm just…I have a headache."

I scrub our plates in the sink, biting on my lip vigorously.

"You look pale, baby." I feel his hand on my waist and exhale when his other one rests on my forehead. "Maybe you should stay home."

"No, I can't delay going back any longer. I have to work."

"You won't be any help to them if you can't focus on more than a paragraph."

"I'm honestly *fine*, Benjamin. Stop worrying about me."

My panic has finally reared its ugly head, making me instantly ashamed.

"If you'd like to talk about it, come to my office."

I keep a hard gaze on the counter in front of me until the elevator doors close, distancing us entirely.

***

"Darcy?"

I glance up from my computer, finding Danielle

in the doorway. Christ, I feel like the last time I talked to her was my birthday dinner years ago.

"Yeah?"

"Wanna get some lunch? A couple of us are going out."

"I wish I could," I murmur apologetically. I glance at the clock, realizing I'm running late. "I have a doctor's appointment in twenty minutes. I'm really sorry we haven't been able to go out. So much has been happening."

She smiles kindly. "Yeah, I heard about your wedding. Congratulations."

"Thank you. Well, how about we raincheck for tomorrow's lunch? We can get Italian or something?"

"Sure."

As soon as she leaves, I stand, stuffing my electronics into my bag with trembling fingers.

Sitting in the doctor's exam room, I realize they still haven't stopped moving. I settle one hand on the other and clutch my fingers tight, forcing my knuckles white. I've had a pap smear, urine test, everything possible to determine what could be happening.

My head shoots up at the sound of the door re-opening. My doctor enters carrying a clipboard with my information…and results.

"Mrs. *Scott*," she emphasizes the use of my new last name with excitement, "first off, I'd like to congratulate you on your wedding."

"Thank you."

She sits down at her desk with a sigh of finality. "You are pregnant. Your suspicions were correct."

CHAPTER FIVE

I let out a sound. I have no idea what sound it is. I haven't made it before.

"A-Are you sure?"

She nods, regarding me closely. "I'm guessing this wasn't planned."

"No." I'm fighting back tears. "No, I just got married. We've barely had time to be married."

"Unfortunately, I do have more news…important news."

I wait, terrified.

"You are anemic, Darcy. Severely so."

"What does that mean?"

"Your red blood cell counts are diminished. A normal hemoglobin count should be 12 to 16. You are currently at 6." Her expression tells me I should be worried.

"What does this mean? Can we do something about it?"

"I'm going to be prescribing you iron supplements. You need to eat well and eat things with a high percentage of iron. Lean beef, oysters, chicken, potatoes, beans, leafy vegetables…I need you to understand that we need to get this back up. Your red blood count cells are equally low, and this is extremely dangerous, for you and for this baby."

"Dangerous?"

"Severe anemia doubles the risk of death in pregnancy, Darcy." I stare at her, struggling to absorb those words. "I'm telling you this to let you know that this is not something to play around with. Anemia of this magnitude can cause stroke, kidney failure, excessive bleeding after delivery, and that's not taking your baby into consideration. Unless we can get this blood count to a safer level, your risk of miscarriage is increased considerably."

I can't believe this. I hold my head, scared shitless.

"Are you understanding what I'm saying?" She waits for a moment. "Darcy?"

"I-I just…I'm trying to think." I have a million questions. "How far along am I?"

"Eight weeks. Two months."

I shake my head. "So this happened right after I got out," I mumble. "I don't understand. I'm on birth control. I saw you a few months ago. Was I anemic then?"

"No, which is why I'm stating the importance of iron to you now. Your pregnancy seems to have brought this on. As for birth control, there is always a slim chance of conception or that you engaged in intercourse before the clear period."

"Okay, so these supplements, they'll help me? Is there a chance I could get worse? What are the symptoms?"

"I'm putting in now that you need one blood transfusion immediately. I don't want to do more because I don't want different people's blood in you, especially during a pregnancy, but it's too risky to let you go home like this. I want you to go today, you hear me?"

I nod.

"Have you been tired lately? Overly tired? Maybe dizzy?"

"Yes."

"I'd suggest taking time off from work if you're able. Rest is paramount for the health of you and your baby."

"I just got a promotion a few months ago…I don't know what to do."

"If you have to work, you cannot be moving around. Tell your boss that excessive lifting, any particular strain, is dangerous. If you need me to write a note, I will."

Two months. Two months pregnant.

"I've been drinking. I didn't know. I was drinking a few days ago."

"That may account for this current result, but I don't think that's what's going on here. We'll need a few days until your blood tests come through to get a better understanding of what is causing this. I'm prescribing you the supplements and nausea medication because we don't want to be concerned about vomiting."

"Is it possible to have anemia and still have a healthy baby?"

"It is possible. All of these measures we're taking are precautions. Necessary precautions, because even if you weren't pregnant, this cell count is not normal. If it is an infection or a chronic disease that is causing your cells to lower, then you will be undergoing a high-risk pregnancy. As of now, this is high-risk. I think you're entitled to know the truth and the risks…as hard as they are to hear."

I take the papers from her hesitantly and clutch them in my grasp.

"We are going to do this together, Darcy," she says with a smile. "We will get this handled. You do your part, and I'll do mine, okay? Having a child is one of the greatest joys in life. I am determined to make sure that happens."

My world is spinning. Her positivity is lost on me. "Am I good to go?"

"Yes, my assistant will schedule your next appointment, which will be in a few weeks if there are no problems with the test results."

"Okay, thank you." I walk for the door, hearing my own labored gasps.

"Call me if you have any questions, any concerns, Darcy. Don't hesitate."

I escape into the bland white hallway like my life depends on it.

***

My palm hovers over the sink, a copulation of pills directly in the middle. I'm holding a glass of water with the other, staring into space, trying to recover from whiplash.

Whiplash hearing that Benjamin and I are

expecting.

Whiplash hearing that my body is rejecting the pregnancy.

Whiplash hearing that my baby is in danger.

This wasn't how this was supposed to go. Benjamin and I were supposed to have time, time to come to an understanding. He was supposed to want this.

I stuff the pills into my mouth and swallow them with a gulp of water. My emails are gathering quickly on my computer screen, and the office is bustling outside my door. I've been sitting here on company time for more than an hour, unable to move a muscle.

My phone vibrates on my desk, and Benjamin's name appears, a photo from our wedding taking up the space around his name. I want to cry, but doing so will unravel me, and I need to remain clear. I need to absorb this and act.

Cindy appears at the door. "Darcy, do you have those manuscripts yet?"

Glad I worked late last night, I pull them out of the drawer and hold them out to her.

She tucks them under her arm and turns, then stops in the doorway and turns on her heels. "Are you okay? You're really pale."

My mouth won't open, and I can't meet her eyes.

"Darcy? Are you okay?"

"No," I whisper.

"What happened?"

"I'm pregnant."

Her eyes widening, she shuts the door and approaches my desk. "How far along?"

"Two months."

"And you're not happy about this? You're newly married. It's soon, yeah, but not unheard of."

"It's a high-risk pregnancy."

She lowers into a seat across from me. "What do you mean?"

"My red blood count is too low. I'm anemic."

"That's usually not that bad."

"It stemmed from the pregnancy, the doctor thinks. She said a normal hemoglobin count is 12 and I'm at a 6. She said miscarriage is possible if I don't get this under control."

"Oh God. What do you have to do?"

"She mentioned iron supplements, a different diet, blood transfusions, rest."

"Can you work?"

"She mentioned time off, but this isn't a physically demanding job. I think I'll be fine for a few months. I'll need to take a leave later on, though."

"We can work with that, absolutely."

I stare at the white gauze around my arm where they spent hours pumping a bag of blood into my system.

"Have you told him?"

"No."

"Honey, you need to."

"He's going to leave me. He doesn't want kids."

Her brows instantly furrow. "He told you that?"

"He said he'd want to be able to devote his time to a child and he wouldn't be able to right now."

"Maybe he'll think differently now that it's actually happened."

"I don't think he will."

"Have faith in your husband, Darcy. He loves you, more than anything. This may be a shock at first, but he will understand."

***

Benjamin's assistant Tiffany is waiting outside her office to greet me, having been informed by the new receptionist when I got off the elevator. That office once was mine, and after the entire walk here that I spent in reflection, it's hard not to be distracted by the sight.

"Mrs. Scott," she says proudly, clearly set on congratulating me. That comes next, and I do my best to fumble through pleasantries. Benjamin's glass doors are fogged, but he's in there.

"Can I go in?"

"He'll be glad to see you. He's been in a foul mood today."

I don't tell her the reason is probably because of me.

"Thanks," I say, rapping on the door gently. I don't know how I haven't had a panic attack yet.

"Come in."

I enter with a gulp. Benjamin's focused on an array of papers covering his desk, glasses perched on his nose, and is typing something into a calculator. Seeing my movement, he glances up and doesn't glance back down.

I wave stupidly.

"Darcy, I've been calling you all day," he says, shooting up from his chair. He drops his glasses onto the mess of work.

"I know. I'm sorry."

Coming over to me, he kisses my forehead and then my lips and nudges my chin up when I try to look away. "Are you feeling any better?"

I shake my head, eying the floor. This is going to be bad.

"No? What are you feeling? Why didn't Cindy let you go home?"

"She did. I've been walking around for a while."

Finally understanding, he straightens with an inhale and sticks his hands into his pockets. "Darcy, what the hell is going on?"

"I went to the doctor today."

"Okay…" He's clearly steeling himself. "For what? Because you felt sick? I could have gone with you."

God, I don't want to tell him.

"You're fucking scaring me," he says, his eyes wide like an owl's.

"I'm…I'm pregnant, Benjamin."

He stares at me for so long with no expression whatsoever that I can do nothing but sit down to wait for his reaction. I have no idea how long we remain in silence before he speaks.

"Pregnant?"

"Yes."

"You went to the doctor today. You found out then?"

"Yes. When I woke up sick this morning, I suspected it then, realizing how long it's been since my last period."

He covers his mouth, shaking his head. "How far

along?"

"Eight weeks."

He runs a hand through his hair. "Jesus Christ."

"I'm so sorry, Ben. I—"

He rounds the desk and takes an abrupt seat, bent as though he's about to stick his head between his legs to keep from vomiting.

"Ben, talk to me. What are you feeling? We need to talk about this."

"Well, what do you feel?"

"Scared, confused…happy in a strange way."

"Darcy…" He swallows, and it seems to echo through the room.

"Talk to me."

"Darcy, we're not ready for this."

"I know. I know we're not."

"We just got married."

"I know." I stare at my shoes, biting my lip. "I know."

His company phone blares, and he picks it up briskly. "I'll be out in a moment." He slams it onto the receiver. "I have a meeting with the investors. They're outside," he tells me, his voice controlled and calm, although I can tell he's anything but that.

"I'm so sorry. I had no idea you were meeting with them today. I should have waited."

"Dimitri's downstairs. He'll take you home."

Tears are at the edges of my lids, near pouring down my cheeks. I somehow manage to keep them at bay. "Okay."

The moment I'm free of the room and the door clicks shut, a bang echoes from inside, and I bite back a sob, seeing a group of men approaching from the other end of the hall.

I need to get out of here.

***

I step into the apartment, not bothering to turn on any lights.

All I want is a bath. After taking another dosage of medications, I strip and settle myself in, relaxing onto the marble ledge.

"Darcy?"

I jump in fear at Benjamin's voice, and my eyes snap open, my hand reactively clutching my chest when I notice his towering form by the door. "Jesus, you scared me."

He's still holding his briefcase. "You were asleep…in the bathtub. You could have drowned."

"Oh. What time is it?"

"Nine."

I slept for an hour in here.

He hands me a towel from the rack, and I haul myself out of the cold water. He hovers by the door while I wrap myself with it.

"What is this?"

I turn, seeing him holding my pill bottle. I open my mouth; nothing comes out.

"Darcy, what the hell is this? Your doctor is already prescribing you medication?"

"It's to keep my immune system up, that's all." I snatch the bottle from him and slam it down on the sink, aggravated by the frustration in his voice. At some point, I'll have to tell him about everything else. Today is clearly not that day.

He follows me out into the bedroom, and while I search for clothes, he undresses.

It's so tense, the air in the room could choke someone. I pick up my nightgown and walk to the bathroom, oddly uneasy to dress in front of him. I pull the soft material over my head, experiencing sharp shortness of breath, panic seizing my nervous system.

Everything was so perfect. And now we're here. I'm changing in the damn bathroom.

I swipe away the tears on my cheeks and force myself back into the bedroom. It takes all the courage I have. He's sitting on the bed waiting for me.

"I'm sorry."

My mouth trembling, I slow down, realizing we've got a big conversation ahead of us.

"For what?"

"For making you feel like you needed to change in another room."

"I'm just as scared as you," I say, hoping I'll touch some deep part of him and magically make him want this.

"We're not ready for this."

"It's happening, though."

"I'm aware of that. I'm just stating the fucking obvious," he snaps, standing up. We're both keeping each other at arm's length, and he furthers the distance, walking to the other side of the room. "Aren't you on birth control?"

"The baby was most likely conceived on that first time after I started taking it. The dates match up, and the doctor said the waiting period between taking it might have not been finished. There's no way to know. I got back on it a few weeks after I got out of…of…"

I can't even say the word.

Saying it would only remind me that this baby is going to be born from an ex-convict.

He remains silent, in his thoughts.

"I'm sorry, Benjamin."

"Your menstruation? Two months? How did you not know?"

"I'm not always regular. Still, I had forgotten." I close my eyes. "It wouldn't have mattered. I'd still be pregnant even if I'd noticed earlier. Are you seriously going to be like this?"

"I'm sorry. I told you my thoughts on children, Darcy, which is why this is a little hard to swallow. I'd like to be the guy who cries and shouts this from rooftops, but that's not me."

"Good to know."

His eyes slant, his face hardening like mine. "We're not getting anywhere here."

"And whose fault is that?"

He chuckles wryly, facing the window. "Jesus."

"I didn't ask for this. I didn't want this right now either. And I expected you to be shocked, and even upset, but I didn't expect this."

"This?"

"Yes. In that tub, I saw an expression on your face that I hoped I'd never see again. The first time we slept together, you had that look in your eyes, and it's back. The idea that you and I are having a *baby* together has made you like this, and that breaks my heart."

He closes his eyes, maybe to hide them from me, to keep me from seeing more.

My cheeks burn from my hot tears. “Look, I’m sorry this has happened and that you don’t want it, but I’m keeping this baby. No matter what it does to me, or to us, I’m keeping it. You can either find a fucking way to accept this or I can go, but I’ll be damned if you bring me down anymore.”

“Darcy, stop,” he breathes when I open the door to our bedroom on my way out.

I refuse to let him witness my pain. I shut the door behind me.

***

I should have known he’d react this way.

I curl my body underneath the covers, unable to find warmth in the guest room. Benjamin is somewhere else in the apartment, or maybe he’s gone out. I haven’t checked to find out.

I slide my fingers over the fabric covering my flat stomach, while reality washes over me, granting me clarification and understanding for the first time since I was given the news.

There’s a baby inside of me.

A baby.

She’s going to depend on me. I think want it to be a “she.”

I need to get my shit together. I need to grow up to ensure this child receives the life I wanted and didn’t receive. Whether she has a mother or a mother and a father in her life, she will find happiness. It’s daunting how quickly maternal instinct has taken ahold of me, how real this has all suddenly become.

There's a tap on the door, then another, and I stiffen. When I don't beckon him in, Benjamin takes it upon himself to open the door. I can see him in the dark, the moon illuminating his shadow. I don't say anything when he passes the threshold or when he places his hands underneath me. Neither do I say anything when he lifts me up into his arms and carries me out of the guest room.

He lowers me onto our bed, and I settle in silently, dragging the sheet up over me. The light in the room flickers off and the other side of the mattress sinks beside me. I tense when his body presses up against mine, his warm chest on my back. He acts as if he doesn't feel my resilience and wraps himself around me, tight enough to hurt.

Emotion washes over me as his lips brush my shoulder, his limbs providing the only amount of protection I've received today. He hasn't said a word, but I'm sure he's apologizing.

He pushes my hair out of my face and kisses the skin there. "I could never look at you like I did back then, Darcy. Never. I didn't love you then."

He laces his fingers with mine on my pillow and captures them, so he can overwhelm me and ensure that I accept what he's trying to give me. At my first sign of submission, a tilt of my cheek into his seeking mouth, he takes advantage and crosses the short amount of space until he can find home to experience the same amount of submission. He expresses his love in achingly slow caresses, his tongue entering me with searching licks. There is no ulterior motive, no rush to take it further. Despite the strain to my neck, I meet his every push and pull, relishing the attention after the day we've had. No anger could surpass this.

"I love you now," he whispers to me. "I could never leave."

My fingers relax in reaction when he buries his face into my neck, losing a great deal of tension we've conceived over the night.

"We don't have to have all the answers right now. We will figure everything out," I say, a noticeable weakness in my voice, hoarse from the tears I've shed.

"We will. I know we will."

I'm not sure whether he believes that or not, but just by him saying it, I gain some of the hope I'd lost.

CHAPTER SIX

I'm not sure why I tiptoe out of bed in the morning. My biological time clock usually doesn't wake me before Benjamin, but today it's dark outside the windows and I'm uneasy, not brave enough to undergo another talk. The emotions from last night are raw, and while we fell asleep a great deal calmer than we expected, I'm frightened of how he'll see this in the morning light. I leave him in the bed, taking up a dominant part of the mattress, his body fully clothed in sweats and a baggy t-shirt, a very unusual sight.

Wishing to get off to work where something distracting can consume my time and force me off of my worries, I take a quick shower and dress stealthily. My husband is still sound asleep by the time I am ready to go.

I should stay. I should lie down and wait so we can dissolve our fears together.

We both acted in panic yesterday, letting confusion rule over our common sense.

I'm closing the door to the bedroom behind me,

my decision made. On a usual day, I'd skip breakfast and head straight to work. Dr. Trigiani's reminders are heavy on my mind, making it impossible to leave without scrounging up something for breakfast.

I make a spinach omelet, and a regular one for Benjamin, aware he won't be asleep much longer. I have no desire to eat a single bite but force it down. Instead of tea, I pour myself a glass of orange juice to wash it down.

I gather my things, set to leave, until I hear Benjamin behind me.

"Darcy."

Shit.

I face him, arching my chin high to hide my guilt. "Hi. I didn't want to wake you."

He's still half asleep, making me wonder if he panicked when I wasn't beside him, which also makes me wonder if I wanted him to feel that way. Right now, he resembles a boy, the traces of sleep etched across his features as he stands at the entrance to our bedroom.

I'm sure my guilt is palpable now. "I didn't want a fight," I correct myself, deciding truth is probably best right now. He's already in the dark about a lot of things.

"I thought we finished that last night."

"I hoped we had…maybe I'm just scared."

He steps closer to me. "Scared of what?"

"What this will do to us."

A safe distance away, I hover by the sink, holding my bag, eyes locked on his by the other side of the island. His face is calm, a wild difference from yesterday.

"Come here."

I set my things onto the counter ungracefully and hesitantly round the table. He meets me halfway, and neither of us slow. His arms envelop me, his embrace excruciatingly tight. I wheeze in a gasp, digging my face into his chest. It feels good to be in his arms.

Wanting to touch his skin, I burrow my hands under his shirt, ascending over the length of his back, appreciating his radiating warmth. I'm cold, truly cold.

"You're trembling," he says worriedly, backing up to search my face. "I know I took it too far yesterday. I shouldn't have—"

"It's not that. I'm just cold."

"Is that a normal symptom of pregnancy?"

I shrug. "I don't know."

"Maybe you should stay home. I could go in for a few hours, take the rest of the day off."

"I can't. I have to go to work."

"Cindy would understand, Darcy."

"I know she would. I like working."

He glances at the ceiling. "All right. Okay, well, will you come home at five then? I can make a reservation for dinner."

"Yeah, I will."

He caresses my cheekbone gently. "Promise me something."

"What?"

"Whether you leave the house before me or vice versa, we tell each other, whether we're fighting or not. I'm used to you being there."

"I didn't mean to worry you," I say, although I probably did.

***

I hang up the receiver, having left Kevin the news on voicemail, too cowardly to wait to speak to him first. My cell blares on the desk. He's going to be pissed about it, but I really can't dwell on it.

"Hello?"

"Darcy?"

I recognize that voice. "Jasmine?"

"Yes! Oh, good! I did get the right number. I just asked Benjamin for it."

"It's great to hear from you. How are you?"

"I'm good. Look, Ben told John...about the baby."

"He did?" I'm surprised.

"Yes, which leads me to this huge favor I have to ask of you."

"Favor?"

"Yes." She chuckles. *"I was wondering if maybe you and Benjamin could babysit for us sometime in the next couple of weeks. We haven't had a night out without Dante yet, and John thought this would be a great chance for you, but mostly Benjamin, to get some practice. He's sure it will be a good thing for him."*

"I'd happily do it. I'll have to ask Benjamin if it's okay but—"

"No need. He said yes."

"Seriously?"

She laughs at my disbelief. *"Well, I kind of had*

to guilt him into it, but he eventually gave in. I told him it would be good practice to see how you two do with Dante. Besides, Benjamin needs to start owning up to his godfather duties at some point."

We hurry through our goodbyes, me because she's pulled the floor out from under my feet…in the best way.

Benjamin agreed.

He's trying.

***

"Knock knock," I announce, opening Benjamin's office door. I smile shyly before noticing another person at the cluttered conference table.

"Oh, I'm sorry. No one was in the front…I'll wait out—"

"Darcy, come in," he says while I hastily try to exit. "We're almost finished."

I'm the shade of a beet, but I push through the embarrassment and enter the room. The man beside Benjamin is short and stumpy and clearly intimidated.

Benjamin rises from his seat when I approach. "Mr. Chapman, this is my wife—"

"Darcy Fontaine, yes." He reaches for my hand with a wide smile.

"Well, Scott now," I correct him as kindly as possible. Benjamin's brows soar, his mouth curving with approval at my attention to detail and the connection we now share. Marriage is a powerful thing. "It's nice to meet you."

"Likewise."

I gesture between them, uncomfortable. "I can wait outside, really…"

"Take a seat at my desk. We'll only be a couple of minutes." Oddly displaying affection in his workplace, Benjamin kisses my hair, which not only startles me, but his employee also.

I choose a random magazine and settle into Benjamin's desk chair while they continue. It ends up being an extreme sport magazine, and I'm deep into an article about snowboarding when Ben stands.

"All right, so Tokyo is out. Send the figures to Singapore. I want word by 8 a.m."

"Will do, boss." On his way out, Mr. Chapman regards me with a parting nod. "Pleasure to meet you, Mrs. Scott."

"Ditto. Goodnight."

It's almost laughable the way Chapman's shoulders slump the moment he's clear of the room, all tension freed by the absence of Benjamin's presence.

"Ditto?" Benjamin teases, in a far better mood than I expected when I showed up here.

I roll my eyes. "Shut up."

He sits on the edge of the conference table while I make my way over to him, remembering the reason I intruded on his day in the first place. He checks his watch, a gift I gave him over a year ago.

"I thought we were leaving to the restaurant from home?"

My lack of response, and the growing smile lighting up my face, should answer his question. I had to come.

"Jaz called you?" he asks, picking up on my cheerfulness.

"Yeah, she did."

"And?"

His eyes close when I'm between his legs, and I sweep my hands over his hair, gripping the nape of his neck. "And *thank you.*"

"I figured it would be good…"

"I know you're going to be a good father, Benjamin."

"That makes one of us."

"Says the guy who spent months by my side without complaint when the worst was coming down on me. Says the guy who knew we were having problems and rushed us to Bali so we could get married and force the problems away." His expression softens. "Says the guy who offers to abandon this profound world he's built because he'd rather be on the run than away from me. You underestimate yourself, darling."

His smile is abashedly pleased. "Keep going and it'll go straight to my head."

"I could go on for days."

He soaks up all the affection I give him, caresses and lingering gazes, thriving on them.

"Darcy, a child is something else entirely. A child is a lot."

"We'll learn together."

When he nods, wrapping his arms around waist, the monstrous weight that had gathered on my chest, weighing me down with uncertainty and confusion, lifts, allowing me a deep exhale of relief.

We're getting somewhere now.

The office door opens with a tap, revealing Tiffany. When she sees me between his legs and our arms around each other, she pales. “Oh, oh gosh. I’m sorry. I didn’t know—”

I try to peel out of his grip, but his hands are locked. “It’s fine. What is it?”

“Your mother is on the line.”

“Tell her I’ll call her later.”

“I did. She’s been extremely insistent. She said she’ll continue to call until you pick up.”

“Fine. Send her through.”

“Okay. And if it’s all right with you, I’m off?”

“Yes. Goodnight.”

“Goodnight, Mr. Scott.” She smiles at me. “Darcy.”

“‘Night, Tiffany.”

When she’s gone, he finally lets me go with a groan. “I’ll just be a second.”

“Do you want me to leave?”

“No.” He answers the incoming call. “Mother.”

I nearly cringe at the formality dripping in his tone. Somehow by the conference table, I’m able to hear her through the receiver, and she is not happy.

“When in the hell were you going to tell me you got married?”

“It’s been public knowledge for a while now.” He begins packing up, phone to his ear.

“I’m your mother! How could you elope and not tell anyone? I’ve been out of the city, and Alexander just told me!”

“My marriage is the one aspect of my life I’m trying to keep private.”

“Private from your family?”

"Why are you calling me?"

I divert my gaze, hearing his disdain. He wasn't kidding when he said they had no relationship.

"You married the prison girl. The girl who killed someone." Benjamin's eyes lock on mine to judge whether or not I'm hearing all of this. *"Ben, come on!"*

That's my name. *The prison girl.*

"Mother, are you trying to get me to hang up on you?"

"Did you even think? This girl comes from no family, and the only family she actually did have was scum of the Earth. Do you even know who you married?"

Although her words sting, I remain unmoving. Benjamin moves around his desk, completely unfazed by her venom. No doubt he's heard this before.

"I know full well who I married," his eyes flicker to me decisively then back to his desk, "and who's carrying my child."

"What? What did you just say?" Benjamin thankfully can't see my horror-stricken face at the drop of our news. *"She's pregnant?"*

"Yes."

"You're having a baby?"

"Yes."

"With her?"

"Yes, with her."

"You've got to be joking…Alex, she's pregnant."

Oh, Alexander's hearing her eviscerate me too. Great.

"How far along is she?"

"Eight weeks."

He shuts his briefcase, not looking up at me.

"Did you have her sign a pre-nup?"

I stiffen as it becomes harder to remain silent.

"No, I did not," Benjamin answers swiftly, blunt as hell.

I hear a shrill snicker. *"Have you got a brain tumor, Benjamin? Have you fallen on your head?"*

Like the night with his father, Benjamin reaches a breaking point, having surpassed annoyance, and leaps straight into fury. "I've had enough of this. No, she didn't sign a pre-nup. We're married, and there is not a damn thing you can say that would change that. Also, since she's heard every word you've said, you may have just lost the chance to get to know your grandchild. Goodnight, Mother."

He slams the phone down.

Now I know why he's hesitant about children. I just heard the evidence.

"Well, she was lovely," I say airily, shielding her insults with a quip, refusing to let her drag us down. Benjamin is visibly relieved to see I've chose amusement rather than complete defensiveness.

"Isn't she?"

I scoop up my purse from next to his desk. "Let's go."

"I'm sorry you had to hear that. She's usually unbearable, but that was disgusting behavior," he says, obviously not past what she said.

Oddly enough, I am. "It's okay, Ben."

Instead of focusing on his mother, I feel for him. Benjamin has dealt with a woman that vicious all his life, and it's a pity. She's never going to know her son, her amazing, beautiful son. I pity her, and one day she'll envy me. She's going to envy that I know him better than she ever will.

He takes my hand as we leave his office and walk through the empty suite.

"What do you think about eating on the boat tonight? It was cold last time we were on it. It will be nice tonight."

"I'd love it," I say, appreciating the world of difference he's made since yesterday.

Noticing my silent probing, his brows furrow while he clicks for the elevator. "What?"

"I love you," I declare, walking past him into the parted doors with a sly smile. I giggle when he catches me from behind and nuzzles into my throat.

"I love you too," he says near my ear as the car begins its descent to the lobby. He's caged me into a corner. His mouth is nearly upon mine when my phone blares between us.

We both exhale, releasing the pent-up tension while I dig for my cell.

Kevin's name is lighting up the screen.

"Shit."

"What?"

"It's Kevin."

"You haven't told him yet?"

"I left a voicemail," I say guiltily.

Benjamin leans into the railing. "Ooh, you are in so much trouble."

***

I rest my elbows against the railing of the yacht.

Benjamin's deep rasp echoes from the bedroom, thirty minutes into a call with someone who's made him upset. My mind is far away, stuck on the fact that I haven't told Benjamin about the medical tests or the fact that my iron count was so low I needed an immediate transfusion. Part of me is sure he'll make a scene about it if I told him. It's why every time I've thought of doing it, I've stopped myself.

There is the option of not telling him, waiting to see if I can fix this somehow, biding my time until we're more secure with idea of having a baby. But this is a secret he will not appreciate being left in the dark on. There are also the dreaded appointments I'll have to schedule around him. I tell myself that I'm doing this to spare him worry, but really, I'm a coward who would rather see him happy about a baby than expecting the worst every day.

We babysit Dante tomorrow, and it needs to go perfectly. It's our first trial run.

"What are you brooding about out here?"

Benjamin's at the door. I hadn't even heard him end the call.

"Nothing important."

"I just spoke to my brother."

Alexander keeps appearing today, doesn't he? "About what?"

"He's leaving Scott Industries."

"What? Why?"

"He's starting a company with my mother. He's decided he is sick of living under my spotlight, that I've dragged him down, etcetera."

"How could he say that? You've given him so

much."

"We've been at odds for a long while now."

"Brothers fight, Ben, but they don't—"

"No, Darcy. This isn't a brotherly fight. We've barely spoken to each other in over a year."

"Why didn't you tell me?"

He doesn't answer me, which instantly tells me that I'm somehow involved.

"It's because of me? Ben—"

"Don't *Ben* me, Darcy."

"I never wanted to drive you away from your family."

"He wanted you. He wanted what was mine."

My heart thumps irregularly at his bluntness, enjoying his claiming. "He didn't know we were together at the time," I remind him with a smile.

"I'm talking about after I fired you."

I stare at him, absorbing the fact that he's kept this from me for almost two years now. "What happened?"

"He told me he wasn't going to stop pursuing you. That he and you had something special and he didn't care about my thoughts on the subject." He sighs heavily. "I had Dimitri keep a close eye on him. Not one of my finer moments, I'll admit. One night he showed up at the bar, but you were off. Dimitri told me, and I went to his apartment…I just lost it. Fucking destroyed him."

I stare wide-eyed at my husband, shocked beyond words.

"I have no remorse for the damage I did to him that night, which should tell you how he behaved. I won't repeat what he said, but remembering it makes me glad you married me instead of him."

"I don't even know him, Benjamin. He and I spent time together that one night at the gala. There was never any possibility of marriage or even a relationship."

"Well, he's fixated now on the notion that he's crazy about you, that he always has been. And that I kept him away from you."

"I can only imagine how angry you were when I told you I saw him at the bar the other day."

I'm relieved when he smirks. "Maybe at him. Not you. I didn't trust you before. It's different now."

"Because you do trust me?"

"Yes."

Yet you're keeping a whopper-sized secret from the man.

He places his hands on the railing and stands behind me, caging me to him. We both hum when his lips meet my cheek.

"Is this normal? Is this what this is supposed to feel like?"

"What?"

"Love. Marriage."

"What does it feel like to you?"

"Secure."

He rests his chin on my shoulder, lacing his fingers with mine on the railing. "I feel like nothing can break us."

"Nothing can," I whisper back, relaxing into his embrace.

***

In bed hours later, I lie awake, tangled in the sheets bunched up at the end of the bed. Benjamin's head weighs down my chest, his cheek against the hill of my breast. The waves rock the yacht back and forth, the moonlight shining off the water and onto my husband's glorious body, which is unabashedly bare.

Catching me by surprise, he moves his arm, indicating he's been awake this whole time too and content in our silence. My pulse speeds as he glides a hesitant hand over my stomach, touching the skin softly.

He lifts his head, laying it down on the arm that was massaging him, his emerald eyes watching me. Speechless, I watch his gaze settle onto his hand on my stomach.

"I've been imagining a boy," he says.

"You have?"

He nods, caressing my skin lightly. "I don't know what to feel about this. At moments, I think I don't want children. I panic, I get angry…then sometimes, when I think…when I think of it being ours and you being its mother, I feel a kind of happiness I haven't felt before."

"I'm scared too, Ben, but we'll do our best. I think we've both experienced enough in our pasts to know what a child wants from their parents."

He turns me toward him so we're face to face. Our bodies flush together, he takes my mouth, tangling a hand into my hair.

"You're going to be a beautiful mother."

***

I untangle myself from Benjamin desperately when I feel a familiar tight sensation in my throat. I scramble out of bed and pull up the toilet seat cover in time to vomit. Unwilling tears blind my vision as I heave, my throat catching on fire.

I've known about the little one growing in my belly for two weeks now, and I'm convinced it's actually making me sicker somehow. Nausea is the devil.

A soft hand pulls my hair back, saving my locks from the line of fire. I want to tell him to go, but my stomach twists again.

Neither of us says anything when straightening, nor when I brush my teeth, avoiding his gaze in the mirror. This is only ten weeks in.

He rubs my back soothingly. "Do you still feel sick?"

I shake my head, and we have no choice but to fall into our routine and move past the abrupt start to the morning. It looks as though we're going to have many more of these. What I'm still not used to is the dizziness that is making it very hard to see straight. With every passing day, I feel a little more off, a little more different than the person I was before.

After a long hot shower to calm my nerves, I'm able to focus on the busy day ahead of me. Doris's house, work, and then Jasmine's house.

"You look beautiful."

I glance up from the vanity, finding Benjamin easing on his watch, his gaze focused on me.

I smile, rolling my eyes. "I don't, but thank you."

My eyes are dark circles. The tan from Bali is long gone, leaving pale, pasty skin in its wake. And my lips are white, a result of my condition. I trace a nude lipstick onto them to hide the natural shade. "I'm seeing Doris today."

"She's no doubt heard by now," he says, smirking.

"Yes, but not from me. I hope she's not upset."

"Why would she be upset?"

He kisses my cheek and picks up his jacket. I don't tell him it's because Kevin has probably informed her of the risks, which I divulged to him when Benjamin wasn't around. She probably is aware that I have a doctor's appointment in a few days, one that will enlighten me as to why I'm in a high-risk pregnancy. I spend the rest of the time Benjamin is in the room staring at him, gearing myself up for a confession I know I won't allow myself to voice.

***

"You and Benjamin will be wonderful parents," Doris says over a cup of coffee, regarding me with positivity. "He's nervous; so are you. Arthur and I were up in arms when we found out we were pregnant. It will pass."

"It's a high-risk pregnancy."

I've focused on pleasantries since I arrived, but it's nearly time to go, and I need her advice. At my confession, she tilts her head.

"What do you mean? What's wrong?"

"I don't know yet. My red blood cells are too

low. The doctor ran tests, and I find out in a few days."

"Is it dangerous?"

"She said many women have it, but usually not this severe. She said it's dangerous, yes, for the baby and me, which is weird. I always thought anemia meant, like, pale eyelids and stuff. There's a lot more to it, I guess."

"What are the treatments?"

"Until we know more, there's not much to do. I'm eating greens, iron-filled foods. I'm taking supplements. I got a transfusion."

"Blood?" She blinks. "While pregnant?"

"Yes."

She takes my hand. "I'm sure everything will be fine, Darcy. What did Benjamin say about this?"

"I haven't told him."

She closes her eyes. "That's…not good. You need to tell him, immediately, Darcy. If this is a risky pregnancy, you need to give him heads up."

"I fully plan to. He's just…he's just getting right with this. You know Benjamin. He's going to freak out and then research the worst stuff and turn this into something bad. I don't want that."

"I get why you've kept it on the down low. But he's feeling better about this, as you've said. You need to tell him, all right?"

"I will. When I know more, after this visit, I *will* tell him. I just want to know all the facts first."

She caresses my cheek with the edge of her knuckle. "You are going to be just fine, Darcy. You both will."

***

I reach over for Benjamin's hand to provide support. Even though he's trying very hard to conceal it, I can tell he's panicking. We're on the way to Jasmine's and John's house. I manage to free his fingers from the fist he's formed and flip it over onto my lap, massaging his skin from palm to jumpy fingers. His eyes never leave the road, but his shoulders relax—a good sign.

John and Jasmine's house looks like them. Warm, beautiful, and larger than life. Out of the way of the city, their mansion is complete with expensive landscapes and Mediterranean vibes. Their wealth is on full display and protected by a towering gate.

"Come on. We're late," Benjamin says, unbuckling his seatbelt. I smile at his nervousness.

I shut the door and take his outstretched hand. "It's going to be fine."

He looks down at me, not bothering to say anything.

I ring the doorbell, and wanting to disarm him, I lift onto my toes enough to peck his cheek. Somehow he manages to disarm me when he cups my cheeks and plants his mouth on mine. I blush, pulling back hastily when the door opens.

Jasmine chuckles and hugs us both. "Hello, you two. Come in. Come in." We enter behind her, and I gawk at the size of her foyer.

"Your home is beautiful, Jasmine."

"Oh, thank you so much. We just finished the remodel."

John walks out, shrugging into his jacket. “Thank you for doing this for us. We’ve forgotten what it’s like to go out on the town.”

Benjamin glances at me, blinking.

“You look terrified,” he says to Benjamin, patting his back with a chuckle.

Benjamin shakes his head. “I’m fine.”

“What are you guys doing tonight?” I ask.

“We’re going to see a play and have some dinner in the city. If we don’t leave now, we’ll miss it…” She glances at her watch. “Dante’s in his chair. He missed his nap, so he shouldn’t be up for too long. I have a bottle for him in the fridge. Give it to him in about an hour and he should pass out after that.”

“Okay.”

“Let me show you his room and changing station and all that,” Jasmine says, taking my hand. I follow her, letting Benjamin relax his nerves with John.

I follow along, listening intently while she explains the routine for the night. I’m sure of myself when we approach the men again.

“Don’t worry about anything. Have fun.”

Jasmine picks up her clutch. “Thank you. We’ll call when we’re on our way back. Text me if you need us at all.”

“Of course.”

I close the door behind them. “You know, I don’t ever think I’ve seen you this nervous.” I chuckle.

Benjamin’s eyes narrow. “Funny.”

“Let’s go see Dante.”

He’s in the living room in a bouncy chair, playing with one of the dangling toys attached to it.

“Hi, you!” I gasp, reaching down. Wide eyed,

the boy blinks up at me with the most gorgeous hazel eyes. I lift him out of the bouncy chair. He kicks his legs, bludgeoning my sides, and I hold my breath while he closely assesses my face. "Hi, Dante, I'm Darcy. This is Benjamin, your godfather. You already know him."

Dante's curiosity is all-consuming, which makes him eager to touch. He paws my face with small grazes, and I relax, pleased when he doesn't cry at the sight of me. Okay, step one.

"We're going to watch you while your mommy and daddy go out for a little while."

"I don't think he's going to talk back, Darce," Benjamin jokes behind me.

"Benjamin doesn't understand us," I whisper, giggling. "You understand me, right?"

He stares at me, bouncing in my arms. Damn, this kid is strong. He points to his toy on the floor, mumbling, "'Pant. 'Pant."

"Oh, you want your toy?" I ask, setting him down. I settle myself behind him, and amazingly, he leans against me, playing with a stuffed elephant.

Benjamin takes a spot next to me on the floor. "I gave him that toy after he was born."

"Jasmine told me it's his favorite. He doesn't sleep without it."

"Really?" He nods, staring at Dante. There is pure fear behind his eyes. I know he's seeing this as if we're fast forwarding nine months with our own baby…what it will be like.

We spend the next hour on the floor, absorbed in Dante and his strange, unfamiliar quirks. He plays, handing his toys to us every so often, until eventually becoming cranky, and I assume it's time to feed him. I heave myself off the floor, finding it amusing that Benjamin is following my every move.

"I'll get it," he says.

When I have Dante in my arms, he begins to mumble, springing his arms out frantically for Benjamin. Benjamin looks from him to me blankly.

"He wants you to take him."

Swallowing an uncertain breath, Benjamin reaches forward and takes him from me, cupping Dante's head gently even though he doesn't need to. The sight of Benjamin carrying a child is foreign. It's also overwhelmingly beautiful. I'm immediately breathless, witnessing raw emotion cross Benjamin's face, and have to retreat to the kitchen to recover from the surging emotions.

I return to the living room with a bottle, screeching to a stop when I come upon Benjamin on the couch, the baby cradled to his chest. He notices my admiring and smiles. I will my feet to work again, walk over, and hand him the bottle.

"What do I do?" he asks when taking it from me.

"Hold it to him. He'll do the rest."

Surely enough, small fingers search for the bottle, and Dante finds a good grip on it. Benjamin is much more immersed in him, looking at the baby with curiosity and intrigue. I flick on the television, which is already set to a children's show, and Dante's attention is secured.

A few hours later, the front door opens. I manage to sit up when John walks into the room. We've already put the baby to bed and also experienced the shrill cry he makes when waking up. I changed his diaper, expecting that would be all.

That was far from the case. It took another hour to get him to lie down in his crib. Every time one of us would think he was calm enough, he'd prove us wrong. It's nearly eleven, and he just went down for the count.

John grins when he sees us, primarily Benjamin, who hasn't roused despite the intrusion.

"Tough night?"

"No, no. Dante was really good."

I touch Benjamin's leg, and his eyes snap open. He notices John and now Jasmine standing in the threshold to the living room, laughing.

"How was the play?" I ask, rising onto stiff legs.

"It was so amazing. We'd seen it before, but it was even better than we remembered." Jasmine sets down her purse. "You guys look beat."

"We're fine," Benjamin reassures them, but they're not fooled. John reaches into his back pocket, removing his wallet.

"Put your wallet away, John," Benjamin says, offended.

John frowns. "Are you sure?"

"Of course I'm sure."

"Well, when you have your baby, we'll return the favor, amigo."

While John hugs Benjamin, Jasmine locks eyes with me, a knowing smile across her lips. And I feel it.

We're going to be fine.

***

"We're home."

I open my eyes, hearing Benjamin's whisper in my ear, and unbuckle my seatbelt. As we walk through the parking garage at nearly midnight, he extends his arm, and I walk into him, sleepily latching onto him for warmth. He smells of peppermint and baby powder, which is an oddly satisfying smell. The moment we step into the apartment, we're shedding our clothes and dropping into the bed without showers.

"Man, I was not prepared," I say after a few beats of silence.

There is a ghost of a smile on his lips. "I second that."

"We did well, though."

"Yeah, we did."

Remembering my medication sitting on the bathroom sink, I have to pull myself back up out of bed.

"Where are you going?"

"Bathroom," I whisper, turning off the bedside lamp. I down the pills with a glass of water, eying myself in the mirror with shame. I set the pill bottle down, thinking of the appointment I have in the morning with the doctor. Fear is momentarily paralyzing, the uncertainty of my condition weighing down my thoughts.

I hope I'm okay. I hope the baby will be okay.

I walk back into the room tormented by a sudden downfall to my nerves. My toes are oddly frozen, prompting me to cross the room to find socks. When I find none in my drawer, I resort to Benjamin's. I choose a pair, slipping them clumsily onto my feet one by one. A small box catches my eye before I close the drawer, particularly the small logo of a pacifier on the top. Hearing Benjamin's peaceful, rhythmic breathing, I cautiously pick it up and lift the lid.

Inside is a small silver rattle, and attached to the end are the letters B & D.

Benjamin and Darcy.

Shocked, I wonder whether it was a gift to him or something he had made. My question is answered when I peek into the drawer again and find a small jumpsuit with Scott Industries printed by the breast. There are two of them—one in blue, one in pink.

My smile is unstoppable. I carefully replace them in the same place I found them and close the drawer, remaining still to soak in the pleasure of the sight.

Benjamin stirs when I burrow into the covers he's already folded out for me.

"You okay?" he asks. I mold to his back and wrap an arm around his waist.

"Yes, I'm fine. Go to sleep."

***

"Again, Darcy. Come again. *Come*," Benjamin gasps against the back of my neck, plunging into me from behind. Before the sun had even risen, we both roused out of sleep and gravitated toward each other. It was a silent decision to begin removing each other's clothing, and we've been anything but silent since. Now the sun is peeking into the windows, and we're drenched in sweat, trembling wildly as we prepare for the second wave of ultimate pleasure.

His hands are firm on my hips, grinding me onto him, pushing himself deep enough to hurt. His tongue is hot against my neck, traveling over the skin concealing my frantic pulse. I'm lost in the building pleasure, sunken into the bedding as he worships my body, his hand under the curve of my jaw. We come together loudly, without reserve, and we've hardly got a recovering breath in before he's pulling me up, spinning me to take my mouth.

He settles onto the bed, and I crawl onto him, dropping my face onto his chest exhaustedly. He sighs when I drag my hands through his hair.

I lift my chin, tilting back to find his eyes when I've recovered. We both smile cheekily.

"Good morning."

He curves an arm around my waist and flips me onto my back, snaking over me predatorily. He hovers above me, his abdomen scrunching into long, thick lines of muscle. "Fuck, I can't keep my hands off you."

Blushing with delight, I give him my lips eagerly, and we devote the few minutes we have left to rough, desperate kisses before he finally has to pull back and climb out of the bed. I make no effort to move, following Benjamin's movements throughout the room, gloriously nude as he chooses his suit for the day, leaving his garments at the foot of the bed.

I'm married to this man.

"If you don't stop looking at me like that, I'm

never going to get to work," he warns without having to meet my gaze to know I'm staring.

"Oh? What are you going to do?" My eyes descend over his chiseled body to his girth, admiring the thick, hard presence between his legs. He could definitely prove his point.

He rounds the bed, slow and calculated to throw my heartrate off the charts, pinning me with a look of lust, with barely restrained desire. My limbs sink into the bed in intimidation. He bends and wraps his fingers around the nape of my neck, urging me to his mouth. My jaw slacks as he tugs on the swollen skin suggestively.

"I'll fuck you against the shower door."

I reach out and wrap my hand around his cock, daring him to do more. My stomach flips when his eyes close and his teeth sink into his bottom lip at my healthy grip.

"Then do it," I dare him.

Always one to rise to a challenge, he heaves me out of bed.

He does good by his vow, devoting his morning to my pleasure. Somewhere along the way his motions soften, his touches becoming sweet caresses. My forehead cools against the glass of the shower, and I'm able to remember a time where we did this, after our first night together. The desire, the need, hasn't changed under the confines of marriage. In fact, it's thrived.

We've found a high ground, one we can love each other freely upon.

One that succeeds partnership and melds our souls into one.

***

My nerves are shot by the time Doctor Trigiani enters her office, her hands grasping her clipboard. The clipboard with my information, my test results. My flustered brain made me late to the appointment, so I've had to wait in her office for her to finish up with another patient.

"Darcy, it's a pleasure to see you again. How are you feeling? You're looking pale."

"I'm okay," I say, wringing my hands in my lap. "I'm sorry I'm late."

"It's quite all right. Now tell me, how has the morning sickness been? Have the nausea meds helped?"

"I've been sick a lot less."

"Good…good. And strength? Still weak? Fatigued? Dizzy?"

I want to lie, but I know she'll see past it. "It comes and goes. I've been taking the pills religiously, and have changed my diet."

Her phone rings on her desk, and she apologizes to me, answering it briskly. "I'm with a patient." Someone speaks to her on the other end, and she nods. "By all means, Stacey."

She's barely put the phone back into the receiver when the door opens and her assistant enters, holding the door open for someone else. My heart lurches to a complete stop.

"B-Ben," I choke out as my husband enters the office, instantly taking all the available air in the small room. His forehead is creased, his mouth set firmly into a line. He's not happy, and rightly so. I realize how badly I've fucked up. I'm rising out of my chair, caught up in my own panic.

"Your doctor was worried you hadn't made it. She called me about your appointment twenty minutes ago," he divulges crossly. He flattens his hand against my spine, urging me to sit. I do it without question.

"Mr. Scott, I'm glad you could make it. Support is necessary with instances such as this."

Oh, Christ. I'm about to be killed.

Ben doesn't comment, probably too confused to understand her wording. I'm eying the door, contemplating a diversion to escape.

"Severe anemia is pretty rare, usually 1 in 100 pregnancies. Your wife is going to need rest, especially going into the second and third trimester."

Benjamin sits forward, and my blood flow ceases altogether. "I'm sorry? Severe anemia?"

The doctor regards us in confusion. "Yes, Mr. Scott. Your wife is anemic."

Fuck.

Dr. Trigiani's eyes flicker to mine in disappointment.

"What is that exactly?" Benjamin presses.

"Her red blood cells have deteriorated. It's a condition in which you don't have enough healthy red blood cells to carry adequate oxygen to the body's tissues. Your wife's case is severe, although the transfusion brought her hemoglobin up to 7.4. Still low, but better, which means after I perform your vitals, Darcy, you may be even higher since you have been taking the medications."

My heart takes a pitfall.

"How dangerous is her condition?" he asks after a moment.

Doctor Trigiani glances briefly at me and then back at Benjamin, gaping for a moment in hesitation. "This is a high-risk pregnancy."

"What is high risk, Doctor?"

"Ben," I whisper, "I—"

"No," he pins me a look so full of betrayal that I shut up immediately. "Doctor?"

"It means precautions are necessary to ensure a healthy pregnancy and labor. It also means knowing the dangers, despite how rare it is to have things go south."

"Could my wife die from this?"

She gapes slightly because it's impossible to not be intimidated by him, especially when he's bristling. "In anemia cases, there's a greater chance for miscarriage rather than death of a mother. However, it's important you know the facts going into this. Anemia doubles the chance of death in pregnancy, because the body isn't receiving the proper nutrients, let alone proper oxygen to sustain two human beings. It's extremely rare, Mr. Scott, and we are monitoring your wife's pregnancy closely."

His hand has bunched into a fist in his lap. "You just said you had to perform more tests."

"Because we don't know what's causing the anemia yet. It's usually due to loss of blood, but she's not losing any. It's most likely a medical condition in her case. We will be scheduling tests, and we will find out what it is."

"Fucking hell, Darcy," he growls, snapping back in his seat. He covers his mouth and stares at me, speechless.

The doctor stands. "I'll give you two some time."

As soon as the door is closed, he's up fast as lightning and doesn't stop until he's by the window. His arms are laced in front of his chest, his back rigid.

"Benjamin, I can explain."

"You kept this from me."

"Ben, I'm sorry, I—"

"You lied. You lied straight to my face. Went behind my back and—"

"I was going to tell you."

He turns on me, seething. "*When*? Before you went into labor?"

"No, I was going to wait until I knew what was wrong. I didn't want to worry you! I knew you wouldn't warm to the pregnancy if I told you. I knew you didn't even want this so I had to make a choice."

"Don't turn this on me. Don't you *dare*, Darcy!" he bellows, and I blanch. "This was your choice, your secret! Fuck, I even asked you what those pills were for, and you chose not to tell me. Your goddamn life is at risk, and I've been playing along to the charade you've made this into!"

"Charade? Are you kidding? Benjamin, I should have told you, I know that. But you have to understand why I hid it!"

"You still want to go through with this? Even though it could mean your death? The baby's death?"

I gape at him, tears rushing to my eyes. "What is the fucking alternative, Benjamin?"

He doesn't dare voice it. I rush to my feet, gripping his arms. He shoves my hands away and clears a safe distance from me. He falls so quiet it becomes terrifying.

"It's strange," he finally says. "The anger I feel right now somehow outweighs the embarrassment of our doctor thinking you have to hide shit from me. You knew this appointment was today. I spent half the morning inside of you and never once did you think it would be nice to tell me about the appointment."

"It's not that bad, Ben. She said I'm improving. You heard her."

"I also heard her say she has no clue as to why you are sick. All I know is that you weren't before you got pregnant, and that is not comforting to me."

"It's a risk. I know that…"

"You could die, Darcy. I could lose you."

I chuckle wryly. "Of course that's what you took out of that conversation. See? This is exactly why I wanted to wait! So you wouldn't overreact!"

"Overreact? Are you fucking crazy? Darcy, you are hearing what you want to hear. I am hearing the reality."

"I'm pregnant, Benjamin. That *is* our reality, and you know it. I know you feel betrayed by me, and you have every right to be angry. I never wanted you to find out this way, but I am sure I can do this. I need you to be in this with me."

"Really? You've been doing just fine without

me," he snaps lividly. I shake my head despairingly as he bounds to the door and throws it open. The lobby is full and attentive to the commotion as I follow him out. Our doctor is by the reception desk, her eyes following my fuming husband storming out of the clinic.

"Ben, stop!" I'm crying now. I've done this to myself, and that makes the tears worse. "Ben, please."

He doesn't stop. He pushes the front door open, taking his keys out of his jacket.

"Please, Ben. Don't do this."

Flashes suddenly light up the sidewalk, paparazzi lined up, having prepared for our exit. Someone must have tipped them off after seeing Benjamin come in. Benjamin's grip is excruciating on my arm as he ushers me to the car on the curb, a ticket sticking out from under the windshield wiper. He snatches it off, his face masked with impassiveness for the cameras. I climb in, eyes on my lap.

He slams his door in their faces as they swarm the car and honks the horn until they move, for fear he'll run them over. He merges into traffic, rigid in the driver's seat beside me. Clear of the cameras, the tears flow freely down my cheeks, soaking my clothes.

"Ben, I'm sorry. Baby, I'm so sorry."

He doesn't answer me, and I continue to ramble, terrified.

"I just didn't want you to worry about me," I say. "I was scared, and I wanted so badly for you to be okay with this."

"So you decided it was better to keep this from me? Did you tell Doris?" His eyes widen, and he looks over at me. "This is why Kevin was worried…this is why Cindy told me she planned to schedule your leave in a few months."

I stay silent, and he curses under his breath. "Everyone knew. Of course they did."

"Ben, my body is strong and—"

"There's evidence in that office that suggests otherwise, Darcy!"

"There's absolutely nothing we can do about it, Ben! You came in me months ago and I got pregnant! Fighting isn't going to change it!"

"You deserve my anger, Darcy. You've had time to process this. I was blindsided by this appointment and by your damn lies, so give me a fucking break."

I fight desperately to breathe. We slow in traffic, stopped at a light. Our silence is heavy and suffocating. He's right, and I know he is. I want so badly for him to be this ray of positive light, but that's not Benjamin. He worries, and he worries about me more than anything else in the world. And a doctor just told him I could die because of this pregnancy.

"I love you, Benjamin," I whisper, needing him to hear it. "I can imagine how upset you are, especially hearing what she said. I know it scared the hell out of me when I heard it."

He doesn't move an inch when I rest my hand on his arm.

"Someday this is all going to be a distant memory. We're going to have an amazing kid, and all of this is going to be something we wished we had handled better. Is this really how we want to spend the next five, six months? In a panic? Or can we embrace this time and appreciate the fact that something you and I made together is growing inside of me?"

"You're only saying this because you're the one on the chopping block," he says. "If things go wrong, it's not you who has to live with it. It's me. You are asking me to get right with the fact that every day you get closer to giving birth, you are in more danger."

"I'm not asking you." He looks at me sharply, and I hold the gaze, unfazed. "We are married and this is our baby. I feel her…or him. I *feel* pregnant, and I like it. I really like it. I know you've begun liking it too."

"I was doing that to make you happy, Darcy."

"Bullshit."

"It's not."

"This is truly the most unattractive you have ever been," I snap, yanking my hand from his skin like he's burned me. Instead of remorse, I'm overcome with blistering anger. "Don't do it for me, Ben. I've lived my entire life trying to remember my father and forget my uncle. The last thing I want for this child is a father who doesn't want it."

His head snaps to me, paling at the comparison. At the sweeping horror that crosses over his features, which he quickly replaces with impassiveness to disguise how greatly my words sting, I experience a tinge of regret.

He's focused on the road, the traffic plowing across the intersection while we wait for the light to change. I keep opening my mouth to say something, disturbed by his silence, but can't find words. I've injured him and I know it. It's rare when I manage to do that, which makes me realize how greatly my comparison holds meaning for him.

In many ways, Benjamin knows my uncle more than I ever did. I lived with him, endured his abuse. I had no idea why he hated me so much. Benjamin knows why, which is something he's never divulged to me. I have no desire to hear it either.

To compare him to that is cruel and untrue. And I'm instantly full of remorse.

"Ben…"

I look at him, prepared to take it all back. His gaze is on the rearview mirror.

It all happens so fast.

The way Benjamin's face slumps with disbelief and then true horror.

The way the car shoots forward without a single nudge to the accelerator, the deafening crunch of an impact surging us into drive, and into oncoming traffic.

The way his arm shoots out to shield me, throwing me back into my seat.

Just like that, the world goes black.

CHAPTER SEVEN

The smell of oil and burning metal fills my senses, stinging my nose with the sharpness. I'm struck by overwhelming pain that makes it impossible to speak. My world is dark, my body immobile, although I can feel the hard cement against my cheek, shards of glass piercing my skin. Sirens are soaring through the air.

My eyes won't open. My head is pounding.

Ben.

"We can't reach them!" someone shouts distantly.

There's a groan near me, and the smell of blood is pungent and overwhelming. I recognize the sound to be Benjamin's, and hearing his struggled gasps, I know I need to move.

He's awake, and he's in pain, his gulps of air accompanied by frightened tears.

I try to force my eyelids open. I try to speak to no avail. He shifts and cries out louder, and I hear a loud clang of glass against the ground. Oil is trickling onto my skin.

A voice I don't recognize shouts so loud I feel like he's in my ear, "Wait, don't!"

***

My eyes shoot open wide at the sudden strike of pain that seems to pierce my brain, a simmering nerve struck at the moment of consciousness. I'm in a hospital. I move to sit up, but strong hands push me down. The noise around me is alarmingly loud.

"Stop, please."

"Darcy, we need to clean this wound. Stop fighting us."

I flinch, clenching my hands in pain. "Where is Benjamin? Where is he? Where is my husband?"

"Mrs. Scott, please, stay still! Lay back. You're not well."

The pain is excruciating.

"Not until one of you tells me where the *fuck* he is!"

I'm pulling my arm from her grasp when my body suddenly freezes, zoning in on the commotion beside me.

I recognize the cuff links immediately. "B…Benjamin?"

The doctors are pressing a defibrillator onto his bare chest. His shirt is open, and what was once a crisp white color is now blood red. I gape at him in horror, terrified by the sight. His eyes are closed, his body thumping off the gurney at the shock of electricity.

In a soft crescendo, my ears begin to accept noise as it is, and that's when I hear the deafening sound of a flat line.

I shake my head, refusing to believe it. Tears spring to my eyes, swarming in a matter of seconds. No. *No.*

"Benjamin?" Fear seizes every part of me. When he doesn't open his eyes, when they land another shock from the defibrillator, I am undone.

God, no.

"Benjamin!" I scream, gutted by a sob. I sit up in a flash, my pain disappearing in my desperation. I shove the girl cleaning my wound hard enough that she slips and falls to the floor. I scramble off the gurney, dropping onto my knees and into puddles of blood to clutch his hand.

He doesn't respond, and I cry out, blubbering in despair. "No! Baby, *no*!"

I've just managed to grab onto him when arms wind around my stomach, forcing me off my husband. "Mrs. Scott! Stop! Doctor, I need a sedative!"

"No! Ben! No! I love you. *I love you*! Stay with me!" I sob, fighting the nurse with all the strength I have. I can't breathe. I can't see anymore. The sobs ripping through my chest threaten to tear me right through the middle, shred me into small, insignificant pieces.

"Doctor!"

"Let go of me! Please! Let go!"

I feel a sharp prick in my neck, and instantly, the drugs drift through my veins, numbing my movement first. My consciousness is coming second. I use the last seconds I have to turn my head to the congregation of doctors standing over my husband.

I black out before I can see him.

***

"Mrs. Scott?" Cold fingers are against my arm. I tilt my cheek to the voice, wetting my lips to try and produce moisture. "Mrs. Scott? Can you hear me?"

My eyelids flutter open, my vision unfocused and blurred. I try to place my hand to my head to clutch my throbbing skull, but an IV makes it impossible.

"Oh no, honey. Don't do that."

The moment I see her, and recognize her to be the woman in the waiting room, the flashbacks hit me like a bulldozer, stealing all breath from my lungs.

I gasp, feeling my lips tremble as I try to control the tears that are coming. "Benjamin…"

"Is *stable*."

I latch onto her words with hope, quite sure I'm actually dreaming. "He's what?"

"Your husband is stable, Darcy. Benjamin is alive."

I choke back a gasp, unsure of what my body wants to do. It resorts to tears, gut wrenching wails that escape me like a flood. I shield my face as she holds me, letting me release and feel the full force of the trauma.

"He's alive?"

"He's alive, Mrs. Scott. I think he's going to be fine."

The sight of him on that gurney, so pale,

surrounded in his blood, is still vivid in my mind, making it hard to believe her words. My tears consume me…for my husband and for the child we've lost. I don't know how I know, but I do.

Maybe it was the devastation of the accident. Maybe it was the strong cramping pain I kept experiencing at the accident scene. But I know she's gone.

"When did I lose the baby?" I ask.

She blinks at my knowledge but answers me clearly. "In the ambulance."

The loss of our baby stuns me, but I'm so heavily medicated, I don't think I can absorb it like I normally would. I stare at the pale white blanket, my cheeks soaking.

"I'm so sorry," she says.

I shake my head, unable to form words.

"Are you thirsty? Do you need anything?" she asks, puffing up the pillows behind me.

"Uh, some water, please."

I take the flimsy cup from her, seeing jagged cuts on my hands through my blurred vision. "I'm…I'm sorry I fought you."

"It was understandable," she replies, checking my vitals.

"I can't remember anything."

"What's the last thing you remember?"

"I was being sedated. Benjamin wasn't alive, I don't think. Everyone was trying to resuscitate him."

"It's the going gossip right now that you brought him back. Even the newspapers have gotten wind of it. He was a complete flatline, and seconds after you touched him, he breathed. With the injuries he sustained, he should be dead."

"What are his injuries? Is he in pain? I need to see him."

"He's asleep. There's no need to worry. What is the last thing you remember before you woke up in the ER next to him?"

"Um, I don't know. I remember sounds, and my head hurt. I couldn't move. I heard him scream next to me."

"Would you like me to tell you? Witnesses have already given statements."

I nod, wincing as I sit up.

"Your vehicle was hit from behind. You went into traffic, and the front of your car was nicked by another going forty-five miles per hour. Amazingly, there were no casualties. You flipped a couple of times."

I don't know if I want to hear this.

"The wreck was severe. You both were caged inside. No bystanders could get you out. A witness explained that he could hear you crying, saying your baby was hurting. He could see you but couldn't pull you out. You were strapped in your seat by the seatbelt, but the car had sunken in to the point that you both were on the ground. Your husband was impaled by a sizeable piece of glass from the windshield. It went through his abdomen, thankfully just missing his liver."

I feel as if someone's struck me. I shake my head, and seeing my fear and confusion, she comes to sit by me on the bed. "You have an extremely brave husband who loves you dearly."

I stare at her, frightened for why she feels the need to say that.

"He pulled out the glass, which was the reason he nearly bled out. But in doing so, he managed to unbuckle you. He got himself out and pushed you toward a bystander."

The last words I said to him light up my mind, bringing me shame.

"That's what the witness said. You were voicing your concern about the baby, and that was when he moved, despite them telling him not to." She smiles kindly. "He fell unconscious before he was able to get himself out, but they managed to drag him out."

My chest inflates and deflates with difficult wheezes as I struggle with the recounting of it all. Benjamin risked his life, pulled the glass from his body to make sure me and the baby would be safe. And he flatlined because of it.

"You arrived at the same time. You miscarried in the ambulance while unconscious. You woke up in the ER, and you know the rest."

"How did they fix the wound? Is he okay otherwise?"

"They moved him into surgery, and they sealed the wound. You both needed a blood transfusion, and he will have more before he can leave the hospital. He sprained his right wrist and arm, but other than cuts from the glass, he's all right. It will take a while for him to recover, not only from the wounds, but from the trauma. For the both of you."

"I need to see him."

"He just got out of surgery."

"I need to be next to him when he wakes up. I

need to."

She tugs on my hand. "You need to take it easy. You've got a sizable gash on your head, and you've just miscarried. I suggest you try to sleep and we'll wake you the moment he stirs."

Frustrated, I lay back into the pillows, forcing myself to remain calm.

"Is there anyone we should call for either of you?"

I nod, giving her Tiffany's number, so she can be aware for press releases and the swarm of calls they are bound to get, if they haven't already started trickling in.

She leaves me so she can make that call, leaving me in a single room, the television on low. There's a game show playing on it in Spanish. The sky is dark, indicating we've been in here all day long.

The events hit like a nightmare, and I begin to cry again, wishing I can forget them.

I don't understand how any of this happened. This morning, Benjamin and I were wrapped in each other, insanely happy. And then we weren't.

It's my fault.

We were hit so fast, and the result was so bloody, so horrific, that it doesn't even seem real. No one person can experience all of this in a day, can they? It shouldn't be possible.

I'm in a hospital gown. My body is empty. My heart is broken. And I can't move. I can't focus on my husband. I can't leave here.

I can only mourn.

***

I squint against the morning light pouring in through the windows when someone nudges me awake. Doris is on the bed with me, her face pinched with concern. I blink at her and once again have to come to terms with the fact that our lives have changed significantly.

"Doris?"

"Oh, sweetheart." She kisses my cheek sweetly, lingering there to sniffle. "Kevin woke me up, said he'd heard about the accident on the news."

"I was too tired to see anyone last night."

"I can imagine." She sets down her purse on the floor. "Kevin is with me. He's signing in now."

"You guys didn't have to come, really."

"You really did bang your head if you think we didn't need to," she scoffs, squeezing my weak fingers.

"Have you seen Benjamin?" I ask. I'm left concerned when she says no. Either no one told me he's woken up or he hasn't regained consciousness. Neither of those warms my heart. Thankfully, she puts an end to the momentary panic.

"He's still asleep. He's been under all night, the doctor told me."

"Did she tell you about…?"

The look on her face says it all. "I'm sorry, honey. I'm *so* sorry."

I cast my gaze down, not wishing to fall into the deep misery I endured last night. I don't have time to dwell because Kevin hurries through the threshold in sweats and a t-shirt. His hair is tousled, meaning he rushed to get here.

"Kev."

"Baby, thank God you're okay." He hovers over the bed to kiss my lips. "How do you feel?"

"I'm fine."

He doesn't look like he believes me. "They're going to release you today."

"And Ben? How long does he have to be here?"

"I believe it will be a week, a few at most. His injuries are going to take a while to heal. I just stopped in to check on him on the way over."

"Is he awake?" I gasp, shooting up. I'll kill that nurse. Kevin nearly shoves me back into the pillows.

"No, he isn't," he says sternly. "You need to take it easy. Doctor's orders."

"How did he look?"

"He looks awful, Darcy. Gorgeous but awful."

But he's alive. *He's alive.*

"I-I need to talk to Tiffany, Ben's assistant. She needs to know what's going on."

"She's been in the waiting room. Want me to get her?"

"Please."

"Okay, we're going to the lunch room. Do you want anything?"

"No, I'm good. Thanks."

They aren't gone even two minutes before Tiffany bounds into the room, her red heels clacking against the tile floors. "Oh my God, Mrs. Scott, I—"

"Darcy, please call me Darcy," I say, mustering a smile.

"Thank you for informing me about this. The news has been playing coverage from the accident on the hour since late last night. They wouldn't give me any news on him as of yet. Is Benjamin okay?"

"No, he isn't. He's in critical condition. His heart stopped for a few moments yesterday before they were able to resuscitate him."

"I saw that on the news. It's true?"

"The flatline part, yes. Me magically bringing him back to life, no."

She chuckles. "People do love a good love story."

"It's seeming like Benjamin's going to be here for a while. I want him to be stress-free, Tiffany. I will assist in any way I can to see he recovers fully. So anything you need, errands, or if you need me to messenger contracts or papers to him and back, I will be glad to do so."

She nods, smiling. "That is so kind of you. With the VP now in Tokyo and no one in the big offices…" She stops her rambling. "Thank you."

"Sure."

"How are *you* feeling? Does it hurt badly?"

I raise a brow in surprise before I realize she's staring at the bandage on my forehead. "No, not right now. I'm fine. I'm being released today, but I'm going to be here with Ben, so call me if you need anything."

"All right, I should be getting back now, anyway. He had a meeting scheduled at ten." She touches my hand awkwardly. "What should I tell the crisis team about this? What should they keep out of the news?"

"Tell them he's going to be back in a few weeks." I swallow, finding it physically hard to utter the next words. "Tiffany, I lost the baby in the accident. I need you to keep that from the media for as long as you can."

She frowns, blinking in shock. "I'll tell the team, and they will do everything they can. I promise. I'm so sorry, Darcy. I didn't know…"

My throat is closing up. "Call me if you need anything. I'll get it to Ben."

That's her cue to go, and she takes it.

It's good to be alone.

I don't have to pretend.

***

"All right, Darcy, sign this and you're free to go."

I take the pen from my doctor's hand and hastily scribble my name on the dotted line. I'm in jeans and a plain white t-shirt and have a bag of necessities that Dimitri dropped off this morning.

"Well, since you will be in your husband's room, I'll pop over later to see how you're doing. After a miscarriage, spotting occurs for about a week. Don't be too alarmed if you see blood unless it's large amounts. If you do, come back and get checked out immediately."

I nod along with what the nurse already told me. I catch sight of Dimitri standing outside the door. "Thank you, Doctor."

"My pleasure."

Despite the situation, a smile forms on my face as I approach Benjamin's most trusted employee. "Thank you for the clothes, Dimitri."

"Of course, Darcy. I wanted to see if you'd like me to drive you back. I didn't know whether you were well enough to stay."

"I'm staying. I'm going to be here until he's better."

"Good," he says, nodding with approval. "He's lucky to have you."

"Thank you."

"Is there anything you need? Food?"

"I'm fine, really."

"All right. Call me at any time, day or night." He pats my arm awkwardly before leaving. The moment he's out of my sight, I walk, faster than I should, toward the critical wing of the hospital. It's a tiring trek. When I reach his door, which has a fake name on the outside to ensure discretion, I'm scared to death.

My eyes zone on him in the bed the minute the door is cracked, and my face shatters along with the rest of me. Benjamin is completely still, bruised far worse than I am. It's apparent he took the real impact of the crash. His arm is in a cast all the way to his knuckles.

Oh, Ben...

It takes me a lifetime to reach the edge of the bed, due to the fact that I can't seem to inch my way forward. I study his wounds, needing to know where he's hurt.

The casted arm is daunting. Although many aspects of the collision are hazy, I clearly remember the strength of his arm crashing into my chest to pin me to the seat. We were fighting and he still thought of me before himself. If I hadn't known the depth of his commitment, I do now.

He'd die for me.

I resist running my fingers over his face, scared to harm him. His skin is scattered with gashes and bruises, dark ones that haven't had the chance to heal yet.

I drag a seat to the edge of the bed and sit, taking hold of his hand. It's warm, and I hitch a breath, pushing away the image of the chaotic waiting room, where I held him and he couldn't respond.

I squeeze his fingers, silently willing him to wake.

When he doesn't, I continue to evaluate his injuries. I uncover him, lifting the gown, knowing the sight of his stomach won't be an easy one. The place he was impaled is bandaged, but there is blood on the gauze. The area around it is swollen and purple.

I'm lightheaded just glancing at it, imagining the pain he must have endured. I swipe under my eyes, but the tears keep flowing, my heart heavy for our loss. I press my mouth to his knuckles, trembling.

"Darcy?"

I lift my head in surprise. With relief, I scramble out of the seat and onto the bed. His eyes are still shut. I gently drag my hands through his dark tangled waves.

"I'm here."

"*Darcy*."

"Yes, baby. Open your eyes. I'm here."

His emerald irises appear through fluttering lashes, forcing a smile onto my face. It takes him a minute to focus directly on me.

"Is this real?" His voice is so hoarse I can barely understand him.

I nod, desperately trying to keep my composure. A large part of me wants to cry like a baby. "Yes. Yes, I'm real. This is real."

His eyes swell with tears at the realization, his lips trembling. I can't stop myself. I lean over him and crush my mouth to his, hard enough that he groans, but he doesn't stop me. I only pull back to apologize, taking the opportunity to do it now when at one point I didn't think I'd ever be able to again.

"I'm…I'm so sorry," I cry. He shakes his head, studying my face. "I didn't mean what I said. I didn't mean it."

"No, I'm sorry. God, I'm sorry," he whispers as I wipe the tears from his cheeks.

"I love you. I love you so much."

"I was so scared it was over." I press my forehead to his, caressing his cheek. "I love you, Darcy, no matter what. I was so horrible to you."

I don't want to think about what we said.

"Are you hurt? Your head…where are you hurt?" he asks.

Hearing the door open, I turn, seeing the nurse at the threshold.

"Oh, I'm sorry. I can come back…"

"No, no, it's okay." I swallow, wiping my cheeks, gesturing her in. Benjamin leans back uncomfortably as she walks to his bedside.

"Mr. Scott, have you realized what's happened? Do you know where you are?"

"The hospital."

"And clearly, you know who she is?"

"My wife," he says, deflating into the pillow. He's exhausted.

"Okay, you will be admitted for at least five more days. We're going to wait it out and see how you respond to meds and some rest."

"No, I can't." He looks at me. "I have—"

"I already talked to Tiffany. We've worked something out."

"I need to work."

She scowls. "You need rest, Mr. Scott. You're not going anywhere."

He glares at her as she checks his vitals and injects more pain medication into his IV.

"On a scale of 1-10, how bad is the pain?"

When he doesn't answer, she laughs and glances at me. "You've got a stubborn one here, don't 'cha?"

Unable to help myself, I agree with her, which earns me a glare from him, although there is no true malice underneath it. He's in good spirits, all things considering.

"Well, you've been asleep for a long while so my guess would be you're going to be very happy when this pain medication kicks in after a few minutes." She turns to me. "The doctor told me to check up on you tonight as well. Remember, if you're spotting, that's normal. If there's more, make sure to find me."

My eyes dart to Benjamin. I cross my arms over my body, chilled to the bone. "Will do."

"I'll bring you some blankets and pillows. That loveseat reclines."

"Thank you."

She shuts the door gently, and Benjamin repeats the question he asked before she disturbed us. "How badly were you hurt, Darcy?"

The fear on his face tells me he already knows. I don't need to speak to confirm it. I know my loss is etched into my very person right now.

He takes a moment to focus on the bedding, and I notice his chest extending wider and wider, like he's unable to catch his breath.

His eyes, reddened around the edges, pierce me, so much emotion barely held at bay.

"When?" he asks.

"In the ambulance."

His face contorts, pained. "I tried to—"

"I know you did. I know you tried to help me."

"I should never have been so cruel to you. The stress…"

I shake my head, refusing to let him blame himself for any of this. "It wasn't your fault."

He swallows, looking unnaturally panicked. I'm not used to seeing him at a loss. "Were you in pain?"

"I didn't know until I woke up in the hospital."

"I'm sorry, Darcy. I know—"

"Can we not talk about it…for now?" I ask. I'm barely keeping it together, and just minutes into our reunion, I'm not ready to tackle anything that happened before this accident.

He's taken aback by my abrupt request, but he agrees.

"Do you remember the accident?" I approach the side of the bed. He's obviously still shaken up about the news I just told him because he doesn't answer me. "Ben?"

"What? Oh, no. I mean, some parts, yes."

"Do you have any questions? The nurse told me a brief version of what witnesses saw."

He shakes his head, closing his eyes. The medication is kicking in. "No, I'm not ready to think about that yet."

"Get some rest. I'll be here."

"No, go home. You need rest too."

"Go to sleep, Benjamin."

"Look who's being stubborn now."

We both smile tiredly, and while the medication takes him under, I watch over him, needing to care for him.

***

"Okay, Mrs. Scott, thank you for your statement. When can we expect your husband's?"

"He's asleep right now. Maybe stop by later?"

The tall, lanky officer nods. "Good day, ma'am."

After he leaves, I walk down toward the reception area, seeing Rose, a senior nurse who is always smiling.

"Hi, Rose. Have the faxes gone through?"

"Feel free to check." She gestures behind her.

I enter her space, walking up to the machine. "Thank you for this. His job is so demanding."

"Of course, everyone knows how important he is. That fax machine is barely used. Feel free to use it while you're here."

I pick up the forms Tiffany faxed over that need signatures from Benjamin. There have to be over twenty forms here…*Jeez.*

"Thank you, Rose."

I head back to his room, knowing he has to be awake by now. It's been over twelve hours. I find the door already open, a nurse by his bedside. Seeing me, he raises a brow.

"You said you'd be next to me."

I roll my eyes, strolling in. "And how are you today, my love?"

His quirky, curly haired nurse scoffs. "Cranky."

"Is that so?"

Benjamin smirks at me, dragging a hand through his hair. He still looks like a model, even with the cuts and bruises. The nurse checks his temperature, inspects his wounds, and sets a tray of food down in front of him. He grimaces, staring down at the food in dismay.

"Eat up," I say, earning a scowl.

"I'd like to see you eat this stuff," he mutters as the nurse shuts the door behind her.

"I've eaten much worse." I shrug, thinking of the dinners in the prison. "I spoke with Tiffany while you were unconscious. I told her I would help getting information and documents to you since she's overwhelmed with work. I hope that's okay."

"Documents? Such as?"

I place the papers into his good hand. He sets the spoon down and scans over them.

"I know you hurt your writing hand, so I figured I could sign for you while you observe me doing it or sign it with your left hand, I don't know. I don't know if that's what you want to do or if you want to wait, but I asked the head nurse if we could use the floor's copier and fax machine and she said yes. I figured you didn't want to get backed up."

He sets down the papers, shaking his head in awe. "I can't believe you thought so much about this…about my company."

"It's not a lot, Benjamin."

"To me it is."

I smile at that. "Well, I need to take a shower and get another change of clothes before I come back tonight. We need to go through these so I can drop them off to Tiffany."

"No, I don't want you to sleep on that horrible recliner again tonight. You're supposed to be resting."

"I'll be fine."

"I'm not the only one that got hurt in this accident. You need rest, a lot of it. You're pale. I know your immune system is compromised. Go home and rest. I'll have Dimitri shuttle these over."

"No, I want to help, Ben. I don't need to sit down."

He huffs, pressing his lips together disapprovingly. "You're not thinking about yourself."

"I don't need to anymore."

I catch my breath, stunned by my own outburst. My chest twists, squeezing my heart painfully. Benjamin's face is pale, his gaze intense.

"Please don't ever say that again," he whispers. I hold my head, berating myself for saying anything out loud.

"Benjamin, I'm not ready to talk about this," I say, my throat constricting at the thought. I glance at him when I receive no answer, finding his attention is set on the wall. It's a while before he speaks.

"I want to take care of you, Darcy, and I can't in this godforsaken bed. So, please, can you try to take care of yourself?"

He looks at me, pleadingly. I'm so madly in love with this man that a simple look from him can cause me to fold. But this—the loss of our child—and the words he said moments before I lost her, are powerful and have sunken deep, despite my desire to move past it all.

He didn't want the baby. It was the last thing he said before we were hit.

And as much guilt I've laid onto myself for the events of that day, those words are still linked to my brain. To hear him ask me to take care of myself, knowing he has no idea what this feels like, causes my blood to boil.

"Please come here," he says softly. I cross the room and take a seat by his legs. He lifts my chin to force my gaze to his face.

I feel my face contort, unmasking my pain for a brief moment. "I can't sleep in that apartment alone…I can't. I don't want to be alone right now."

"You're not alone, Darce."

"I want to go back when you do."

He sighs heavily. "Will you at least spend the nights at Doris's? I know she'll say yes, and at least you'll be on a bed."

"Can you stop trying to get rid of me?" I scoff, which makes him chuckle.

"That's the last thing I'm trying to do. I'm trying

to keep you healthy. Lord knows you won't do it on your own."

I point at the first piece of paper.

"You are honestly the most stubborn woman," he grumbles, with no choice but to lift the document.

"Get used to it."

He smirks. "I don't think that's possible."

***

A gentle hand glides over my hair, stroking it softly, and that is how I come to consciousness. Opening my eyes, I realize where I am. After a quick shower and a shuttle to Scott Industries, where I dropped off an assortment of signed documents, I came back to find Benjamin asleep. I lift my head off my arms, realizing I passed out. He's watching me with a calm expression. I lean into his caress when his fingers nudge my cheek.

"How are you doing?" he asks. "Honestly?"

I don't know what to say. I don't know how to say it. My emotions are so fluctuating. One moment, I'm angry. The next, despairing.

"Talk to me. Please, Darcy. I feel like we need to talk about this."

"I don't know what to say," I utter lamely. "I just wish it hadn't happened, you know? I-I felt her, or him, whatever they were. I didn't know about it for long, but I felt like something was growing in me. I feel empty now."

"When I was in that car and I could barely see straight, I kept thinking about it…about the baby. I don't know why, but I didn't want it to hurt. It's ridiculous considering how I acted from the moment I found out."

He leans his head back, squeezing the bridge of his nose with his unharmed hand. "I'm ashamed of myself. I think about what I said, how much of it I didn't mean, and I want to be sick. If I hadn't stormed out of there, we wouldn't have been on the road. None of this would have happened."

"Stop. We could have handled things very differently, Benjamin, but the miscarriage was because we were in a car accident. None of that blame falls upon you."

I'm trying to make him feel better. I doubt I succeed, because just as he wishes to blame himself, I'm doing the exact same thing, wondering if it was my body that gave out or the stress of our fight that did it. I'll never know, so it's easier to blame the accident.

"You died in front of me, did you know that?" I whisper, wanting to change the subject. His gaze softens when I take his hand. "I did this…and there was nothing. You were gone."

"The nurse told me. She said my heart started again when you touched me."

"Nurses are romantics."

"I don't doubt it for a second," he says, lifting my chin, making my heart stop. His eyes are piercing. "I don't doubt it. You own me. You completely own me. I'll always come back, Darcy…always."

I clutch his face, nodding. He presses his lips to mine, raising a hand to my hair. I feel pain when he tangles his fingers into my waves, but honestly, I couldn't care less.

"Lay down with me."

"No."

"Please," he murmurs against my lips, nodding.

"You'll hurt yourself. Your stitches…"

"I'm fine." He winces slightly, scooting over, and I glare at him beneath my wet lashes. He lifts his arm, and I settle down beside him, careful to not move him too much. Both of our bodies relax against each other, a small normalcy after days of chaos.

***

After a quick scan of the assortment of breakfast foods lined up in the cafeteria, I choose a container of fresh fruit and a yogurt, only eating because I'm drained, and I feel it, which must mean I'm below par on my iron.

"Hello, Darcy."

My entire body stiffens with discomfort. Please, no. Not today. I refuse to even look to my left. "Hello, Alexander."

Lifting my tray, I leave my place by the counter and find a seat, sighing loudly when Benjamin's adopted brother follows me and takes the seat opposite from me.

"You look exhausted."

I open the yogurt carton in silence. He watches me the whole time. "Are you going to watch me eat this or do you have something to say?"

"I don't understand why you're angry at me. Did I do something to upset you?"

"I'm just not in the mood for chit-chat today. I'm sorry."

"I understand. I wanted to see how you were."

"I'm fine."

"The baby is well too? My mother told me a couple weeks ago you were pregnant. I couldn't believe it."

The blows keep coming. I stare at him.

His face actually twists with something resembling regret. "Damn."

"Why are you here?"

"My mother came to see Benjamin."

I'm immediately worried. God, she can't rile him up. He needs rest; he needs to remain calm. I shake my head, furious. "Why is she here?"

"Because she's his mother."

"No. No, a mother doesn't treat her son like an abomination for years. A mom doesn't do that."

"Look, I honestly could give two fucks what goes on between them. I'm just standing in the backlines."

"And that makes you just as bad as her."

His features contort angrily, and I actually feel my pulse quicken, surprised his naturally beautiful face can turn so ugly. "That fucker attacked me because of you. Did you know that?"

"Yes. I do," I snap. "Why would you even act like you care about me? You don't! You're just trying to drive away the only decent family you actually have!"

"Decent? *Decent*? You know what your fucking husband used to be like? He was just like me. He didn't want attachments; he wanted to fuck. You were the first woman I actually pursued, and he felt the need to take that from me too! It's always been a goddamn competition with him, and I'm tired of coming out second!"

"I was his the *second* he laid eyes on me, Alex." I move closer so he can hear me better. "You didn't have a chance. We started seeing each other almost immediately after I started working there."

"You felt something between us. I know you did."

"I don't know you!" I scoff, gesturing wildly with my arms. "I don't understand why you're doing this. I married him. There's no chance anymore."

"There's always a chance you'll see the light and realize."

"I'm not some fucking prize to be won. All you'll be able to offer someone is lifeless orgasms and momentary excitement until you grow the hell up. Benjamin and I are in love. There is a history there that is irreversible."

"You don't know what I can offer. You don't know a thing about me."

"Exactly!" I stand up, walking to dump out the food. I'm not hungry anymore.

"I don't deserve your hate," he growls, his fists clasped together tightly on top of the table.

"I don't hate you, Alex. I'm disappointed. If you'd just get over this fucking competition and keep the job Benjamin has provided you, you'd see you actually have an amazing brother who has been burdened with the same parents as you, who has a lot more in common than you have ever realized."

"He has *never* been my brother."

I bite back insults and try to think rationally. "I'm really sorry they were so cold to you after Daniel died. Benjamin told me. Your family is so fucked up. The loss of Daniel is still hanging over every single one of you. I wish you all could see that and try, just *try* to regain some of what's been lost. You do have a brother, Alex, if you want one."

I stand up and leave him there, glad he doesn't follow me. My blood is pumping from the altercation in the cafeteria. I hurry back to Benjamin's room, afraid of what I'll find. I slow, seeing the door halfway opened, already able to hear low whispering.

"You should go. I don't want you upsetting Darcy."

"I'm your mother. I have a right to be here."

"Do you? When did you suddenly start caring about what happens to me?"

"You know I love you, Benjamin."

He chuckles.

"Why are you laughing?"

"What do you want?"

"What do you mean? I'm here to take care of you."

"I have Darcy for that. Why are you here? What do you want?"

"Oh come on, you really think I wouldn't come—"

"How much? How much do you need?"

"Benjamin!"

"*How much*?"

There's a long pause, and I sink into the seat

outside the room, anticipating the worst.

"A million."

I almost miss the chair. *Dollars*?

"This is for the business you and Alexander are starting?"

"Yes."

I wonder if Alexander even knows that Benjamin is once again going to be fueling his career. Jesus, these people…

"What would I be investing in?"

"Well, you see, Alexander doesn't know you're helping. He's quite set on doing this himself, but he just doesn't understand how much it takes to form a company."

"So you're saying I'd be gifting this money?"

"Yes, that's what I'm hoping. Benjamin, I know I should have been there for you more growing up, but you've never denied me anything. You've been so good to me through the years. Please, I know this is going to take off. The market for seafood is extremely high right now."

"Alexander is never going to learn anything unless you stop feeding him the notion that things in life come easy."

"I know. I'm just trying to get closer to him, Benjamin. I'm trying to get closer to both of you."

Bull-fucking-shit.

"While I appreciate the notion, whether it's real or not, it's unnecessary. I'll have Tiffany wire you the money."

Running my hands over my face, I have to inhale deeply to keep myself from going in there and forcing her out. The man was on his deathbed a couple of days ago, and she's here asking him for money.

"Darling, thank you. I knew you'd be there for us. You always are."

It's amazing how caring she sounds when she wants something. Anger simmers beneath my skin at the thought that he's done this for her before.

I stand up, suddenly very ready to meet her. Pushing open the door, I flash my full set of teeth, wider than necessary. Benjamin smiles softly, looking down. He knows I was listening.

"I'm Darcy," I announce, stepping in.

His mother is not what I expected. I expected her to be a blonde beauty, entirely made of plastic. Instead, she's resembles a conservative housewife with a dull shade of white hair. She's in a blue suit, a white designer bag on her arm. Her hands are French-manicured and dangling daintily mid-air, and I doubt they've ever seen a real day of work. She's clearly old money. Her intense eyes rake me from head to toe, taking in my disheveled appearance.

"Ah, hello," she purrs, turning her attention on Benjamin momentarily before she can bestow it upon me. "Finally, we meet."

Finally?

As far as I know, she's dreaded the day of meeting the "prison girl" for some time.

Alexander walks into the room behind me. It doesn't slip past me that Benjamin stiffens noticeably at his entrance, and by the way Alexander instigates him, touching me so he can get around my body blocking the doorway, he looks seconds away from leaping from the bed.

"Benjamin."

"Alexander."

Alex plants himself beside his mother. I avoid Alexander's steady gaze. He's a jerk for doing this, making it so noticeable something's happened.

"Glad you're all right," Alexander says to his brother, lacking enthusiasm.

"Thank you."

"We have an appointment in thirty minutes, so we should probably get going," his mother says, stepping toward Benjamin. I nearly stop her. I'm angry enough to. She leans in, touching his cheek, and presses a kiss to the same spot. He tilts his face away from her forced affection, glaring at the wall.

My hands are balled into fists at my sides.

"We'll get together sometime." She looks at me. "All of us."

Alexander opens the door so they can exit, and before I know it, my legs are pushing me forward after them.

"*Darcy.*"

Ignoring Benjamin's warning, I shut the door firmly behind me. Alex and his mother spin at the definitive sound.

"Do you even know what he went through in that accident? Did you even ask him?"

His mother hardens instantly at my tone. "He is all right now. That's what matters."

"Your son *died* on a gurney two days ago!" I seethe, horrified by her detachment to a child she birthed. "He has fifty-two stitches on his stomach! Do you not even care?"

"*Died*?" Alexander asks, looking between us. "What do you mean?"

"He flatlined, and by some miracle they were able to bring him back. You almost lost him, and yet you don't even *know* him. Either of you. All you care about is what he can do for you."

"You have no idea what you're talking about. You don't know Alexander or me, and frankly, you probably don't even know your own husband."

Benjamin's nurse walks by, her head low to the floor. I'm sure she's listening. "I know everything about him, and what's more, I love him for him. Not for his money, not for his status. *For him*."

"Look, you're having my grandson. I don't want to say something to you I'll regret," she says through thin, frail lips.

"*Mother*."

She glances up at Alexander's mortified expression and scrunches her face in confusion. "What?"

He whispers in her ear to divulge my unfortunate news, and her eyes flicker to me when the reality sets in. I lift my chin, refusing to be affected by her hollow words.

"Ah, well, I am sorry about that."

"No, you're not."

"Just mind your own business, Darcy. You may be my son's wife, but that doesn't automatically make you a part of this family."

She turns, making her way to the elevator without another word. I don't even have the energy to call out to her. Alexander drags a hand through his blond, tousled mess of hair, appearing ashamed.

Needing to cool off, I pass Benjamin's room and drop into a chair with a huff. My blood is racing, my hands trembling in my lap. Facing his mother was no easy feat, but I'd never have forgiven myself if I didn't stand up for him.

When my flushness has dissipated and my pulse has diminished to a healthy rhythm, I trace my steps back to Benjamin. He opens his eyes when I enter and stares at me. There's no glower, no anger anywhere on him, so I approach his bedside and take his hand.

"How are you feeling?" I ask, noticing the dark circles surrounding his eyes.

"I'm fine, Darcy. I'm not dying. You know that, right?"

"I'm just worried. The nurse said the wound was looking brutal this morning."

"It's fine. It's supposed to look ugly. It's going to scar…so are the scars from the defibrillators. They're permanent."

I press my lips to his cheek as tenderly as I can. "I don't care."

He regards me fondly when I pull back. "I know you don't."

I sit down on the edge of the bed, rubbing his leg.

"You shouldn't let my mother get to you."

"I just hate seeing someone use you like that."

"I'm used to it." He smirks, taking my hand. "When I was shot, years ago, she didn't show, so I figured this time she wanted something. She's easy to read."

"But a million dollars…why didn't you say no?"

"Because a million dollars is nothing to me, and if it gets her off my back *and* yours, it will be worth it."

"And you tell me you're not generous."

"You know, you're pretty sexy when you're fighting over me."

"Yeah?" I'm sure I'm glowing. "I thought you'd want to kill me."

"No. I'm lucky you care so much about my feelings, even though you shouldn't, at least when it comes to them."

"They are your family. You'd think it would be common sense to ask, you know, if just *maybe* you got hurt in that accident. I mean, you've been here for days…obviously something happened. How could they not even—"

"You're rambling."

I smirk, attempting to compose myself.

"I'm guessing Alex saw you before he came in."

"Yeah, in the cafeteria."

He waits, and when I don't expound, he licks his lips, smiling secretively. "You're not going to tell me."

"There isn't much to tell."

"Well, did he bring up what we spoke about the other day on the boat?"

"Yes."

He waits patiently. I roll my eyes and continue.

"He brought it up, and I told him what I told you…that I don't know him and he doesn't know me and that I'm married to you and there is nothing he can do that would change that."

"He actually asked if there was still a chance?"

I shrug, knowing I should have omitted that part.

"I see."

"I think he got the point."

"Well, by the way he was staring at you in here, he didn't."

"Well, there isn't a chance, so I don't want you overthinking this. Leave it alone."

He kisses my hand softly. "All right."

***

I stand up, stroking Benjamin's hair, staring at his relaxed, unmoving features. The medications they give him really put him under within seconds. I decide to use this time to leave for a shower and to change my clothes, maybe finally eat something today.

Upon seeing me, the attendant smiles, pushing the button to summon the penthouse elevator. "Darcy, I hope you and Mr. Scott are doing well. I was worried when I saw the news."

"We're okay. Thanks for asking, Victor."

"Of course. If you need anything, let me know."

I ride the elevator, relishing the silence. I've tired of hospital rooms. I can hardly keep eyes open, my body worn out from constant movement. I will my legs to work when the silver doors part open. As I move through our apartment, I unscrew the cap to the pill bottle, taking out two tablets. I don't know if they are working, but I don't want to take my chances.

I get a water bottle from the fridge and head toward the bedroom, setting my bag down with a sigh. I undress fast, wanting to be back before Benjamin wakes.

The room is unbearably cold when I shut off the water and step out of the shower, unnaturally cold. I wrap the towel tighter around me, concerned by how fiercely I am shivering. I take a long-sleeved shirt and jeans from a drawer and lay them out on the bed.

Within seconds, the room is spinning. I fall to my knees, and everything blurs.

CHAPTER EIGHT

"Darcy."

I feel a hand on my face, pushing my hair from my eyes.

"Darcy, can you hear me?"

Dimitri is looking down at me with wide eyes. I quickly realize I'm wrapped in only a towel. "Wha—"

"You fainted."

I sit up, steadying myself on the mattress, careful to cover myself with the towel.

He helps me sit. "You're extremely pale, Darcy."

"I don't feel very good right now," I whisper, noticing how badly I'm shaking.

"I'm calling a doctor. Where is the number? Do you know it?"

I point to my bag. He takes out my prescription bottle and notes the number, tapping the digits onto his cell phone.

"Hello? Doctor Trigiani? I'm the security for Mrs. Darcy Scott." He nods. "Yes, I just found her unconscious. She's awake now, but she doesn't look well. She's shaking extremely bad too…Yes. Yes. Okay. Thank you."

He hangs up, tucking his phone back into his pocket. "She's coming."

He opens my drawer, taking a nightgown from my delicates drawer. My arms have numbed, and I can barely move them. He notices my rising panic at the loss of function.

He turns around, holding up the black garment. "I can help you, Darcy. It's all right."

He lifts the material over my head, pulling my damp hair through the neckline. I'm grateful as he holds up my arms and guides them under the straps. He positions his hands under my arms, lifting me up enough to move me back against the headboard.

"Do you know why you fainted? What are you feeling?"

"It may be the iron deficiency. I don't know. I've felt fine."

He nods, covering my body with the throw at the end of the bed.

"How did you know I was here?"

"You've been gone for a while. I've been calling for hours. Benjamin's worried sick."

"Please don't tell him."

"Darcy, please don't ask me to do that."

I don't have it in me to fight him right now.

Apparently I drifted off, and I awake when a cold hand touches my forehead. It's Doctor Trigiani, dressed in casual attire.

"Hello, Darcy. Dimitri tells me you fainted. How are you feeling?" She reaches into her bag. "You're running a fever. I have you hooked into an IV.

You've been staying in the hospital, I hear? You were supposed to be resting."

"I know."

Dimitri appears in the doorway, holding a bag of take-out. He removes a container of soup.

"When will I be okay to get up?" I ask as she presses her fingers to my wrist, checking my pulse.

"Oh, you'll be on bedrest for a few days."

"No."

"We're not negotiating this, Darcy. You are being stubborn, and it's clearly doing you no favors. Now, if you get any worse, go to the hospital, all right? If not, I'll check on you in the morning."

I hear an uncomfortable grunt next to me. Dimitri has a phone in his hand and is extending it to me.

Great.

I take it, preparing myself. "Hello?"

"Dimitri just told me what happened...Christ, Darcy! You said you felt fine!"

"I did. Benjamin, it's okay, I—"

"I managed to get the doctor to agree to release me tomorrow."

"You don't need to do that, honestly."

"Yes, I do. You're obviously incapable of taking care of yourself."

I narrow my eyes, surprised by his hostility. "You're being a jerk."

"Well, I'm worried sick. My wife has refused to give a shit about herself."

"You're blowing this out of proportion," I huff as the throbbing in my brain intensifies, plummeting my mood considerably.

"Well, stop hiding things from me and I will be able to calm down. Hearing my security found my wife naked on our bedroom floor, completely unconscious, has me just a little stressed out."

"I'm getting off the phone now." Dimitri's eyes widen when I end the call, making me re-think my decision to hang up on my irritable husband, but after the days I've had, and the lengths I've gone to fake being happy, I'm in no mood for a lecture.

The phone rings almost instantly, and Dimitri bristles with worry.

"I'm not talking to him while he's like this, Dimitri. Please tell him I'm going to sleep."

"Darcy—"

"Please tell him."

He answers the phone, his voice lowering as he exits the room, shutting the door. Under doctor's orders, I eat and endure the aspect of sitting still in my own thoughts.

***

I don't even remember falling asleep. The sky is black, lacking any visible stars. I gawk, amazed I slept the entire day. Sitting up, I reach for the glass of water by my bed, draining it in one gulp. My body is drenched, my bones weak.

There's a note on the nightstand.

He's called three times. Have pity on him. He's calm but worried.

Dimitri

I lift the new phone Dimitri's replaced after mine was destroyed in the accident and dial Benjamin's number. It goes straight to voicemail.

"Hi, I've been asleep. Dimitri said you'd called quite a bit, so here I am, calling you…um, call me back."

I hang up and push onto my hands to sit upright.

"Oh no, you don't!" Doris is at the entrance to the bedroom. She's holding a magazine, but she drops it onto the desk and makes her way over to me. "You're not supposed to be out of bed."

She fixes the pillows, pushing me back against them, and I groan. "Please, I feel gross."

"You spiked a fever just two hours ago and threw up more than I believe is normal for a person of your size. You are not to move from this bed until the doctor gets in tomorrow."

She rests a hand on my forehead, making a face of disapproval. I'm getting it from all sides today.

"I have to take a shower, Doris."

"I have a washcloth."

I'm boiling and want to be left alone.

"Don't give me that look. God, you're stubborn when you're sick."

"Please, Doris. My hair is sticking to my face. I don't want Benjamin to see me like this."

"There's a good chance it will look like this anyway."

"Please."

She eventually gives in and helps me out of bed. In the bathroom, I hesitate briefly before stripping. I climb into the water, knowing it's lukewarm, but to me, it's as if I've plunged into a frozen lake. I wrap my arms around myself and try to endure it.

Doris helps me wash. Her fingers lightly touch my scars, and my spine snaps straight. She notices my unease and removes her hand, continuing.

I stare at the water, reveling in my own pity.

"You've had it pretty rough, rougher than most," she finally says.

"It never stops. The blows keep coming."

"It won't always be like this, darling."

"I don't understand how one minute she could be completely fine, and the next minute, I'm empty and she's just…gone. I don't get it."

"Honey, this is going to take time to process and heal from. Everyone knows how hard this has to be for you. Talk to Benjamin. Take comfort from him."

"I can't talk to Benjamin about it."

"Why not?"

"Because he didn't want her. The last moment I had with her was in a fight with him, when he told me he was playing the role of excited father to make me happy. I can't talk to him and hear him speak like he wanted our baby."

"I got a call today from a department store just outside of the city. They had received an order for items purchased by Benjamin and were trying to reach him to confirm the address for shipping."

"What items?" I ask, hope ringing through the question.

"A crib, a changing table, toys…" She nods when my face falls. "He was furnishing a nursery."

Delirious and exhausted, my eyes burn with tears. I don't want to cry anymore. She lets the news sink in and allows me some time to grieve.

"Benjamin's spent his entire life alone, Darcy. I know this. I worked with him. He never received love from his parents, and his siblings all have their own problems. He has no real aspect of family. You are the one person he's latched himself to in every way. He chose *you* for his family. He's not going to want to risk that for anything, even for a baby."

She massages shampoo into my hair gently. "I think you both are going through something, something completely different. I don't think it's that Benjamin doesn't want a child…I don't think he believes he *should* have one."

He's said that before.

"Besides, a man doesn't buy out a toy store unless he wants a baby. I've seen enough life to tell you that."

She kisses my cheek maternally.

"*Talk to him*, darling."

***

I miss you.

I summon the courage and send the message to Benjamin, clutching the phone, waiting for a reply. I'm not even sure I'll receive one. Not even a minute later, my phone pings.

I'll be with you soon.

Clearly, our argument isn't over. I set the phone on the night table and curl up under the covers, unused to the empty space beside me. I fall into my thoughts, imagining if he'd never been revived in that hospital.

This bed would always be empty.

I'd always be staring into space.

I'd have lost my heart.

Simply thinking of a life without him is enough to irregulate my heartbeat. I shoot my hand back out for the phone, and this time I dial him, holding the phone to my ear.

"Yes?" he answers, his voice full of frustration and a minuscule hint of amusement.

The sight of him on that gurney, covered in his blood, consumes my mind. I try to think of something to say, an apology. But none of that feels right.

"What is it?" he asks gently, knowing he hasn't lost me.

"I love you," I whisper thickly, wishing I could erase that memory from my mind. Out of all of them, I wish I could get rid of that one.

I hear his breath catch. *"I love you too."*

***

Despite how bad I feel, when Benjamin enters the apartment, I leap up from the couch. He's dressed in a gray t-shirt and jeans, his long locks concealed by a baseball cap. Dizzily, I cross the room, feeling oddly childish.

We stop, body to body.

He smiles. I smile.

"I'd kiss you if I could," he says, his mouth widening. His multi-colored bruises are starting to fade. I lift onto my toes, and he tilts his cheek into my kiss.

"You're warm…you still have a fever?"

I take the overnight bag from his shoulder. "It's manageable," I say. "I feel much better."

"Please tell me you've been resting."

"I've barely left the bed, Ben. I promise."

He's walking well but slowly. He has to be careful. It's nearly noon, so the sun is at full strength, illuminating the bedroom.

"Do you need help with the shirt?" I ask when we're by the bed.

He eyes the shirt and nods. "If you could."

I'm lifting the material carefully when he asks, "Are you working?"

The open manuscript is on the bed. I smile, guilty. "I'm doing it in bed, Ben. It's fine."

"Not while I'm here."

"Didn't plan on it." I stand on tiptoes to get the shirt over his head. He grimaces then steps out of his jeans himself, turning down my offer of food.

"I really just want to sleep," he says. His eyes are black and blue, but I can tell he's exhausted by the way his body is slumped. The bandage is plastered across his abdomen, reminding me of the impaling story the nurse said, and I shield my gaze so he can't see how affected I am by it.

It hurts him to get into bed, clearly, but he braces through it silently. I'm more at ease when he's down on his back. I close the manuscript and set it on the night stand.

"I want you here with me," he says, demanding my time.

I smile softly, staring at him. "Is that so?"

"I've had a week without you in my arms. I don't want another second."

His words fill my broken heart with love and admiration. I ease onto the mattress so as not to jostle him and crawl over to his outstretched arm, lowering down beside his body. He circles my back and pulls me into his side.

I cover his leg with mine, resting my cheek into the nook of his arm.

His chest is scattered with scars from the defibrillator, and I can't help but study them. They are a new part of my husband.

"You are burning hot," he says sleepily.

I giggle. "I can move, Ben…"

"Go to sleep."

I don't. I watch him, allowing myself a moment to relax, because he's home, and he's alive.

***

"I've never felt so lazy in my life. This past week has killed my body," Benjamin complains as I switch through channels on the TV. Neither of us wants to watch anything, but there's nothing else to do.

"It doesn't look too bad to me."

"You are the best ego booster."

I press my lips to his warm pec. "I'm here all day, every day."

The rest of the day consists of absolutely nothing. We're in and out of sleep until the sky becomes dark. Now wide awake, I glance at the clock. It's 8 p.m.

I'm in the bath when Benjamin fills the doorway to the bathroom, stunning me that he's out of bed.

"You okay?" he asks.

"I'm good. You shouldn't have gotten up. You could have hurt yourself."

He smirks and lowers the toilet lid to sit down. "I believe we're getting a glimpse of what it would be like to grow old together," he jokes, clearly in pain.

"God, let's hope not," I say. "I couldn't sleep anymore. It's frightening how much I've slept in the past couple of days."

He nods. "My sister is in New York. She just called."

I perk up. I love his sister. "Really?"

"Yes, she landed about an hour ago. She heard about the accident on the news and is pretty ticked off I didn't call her about it. She's getting situated in the hotel and wants to come by tonight."

"Okay."

"Are you all right with that? I know you're probably not up for company, that you're tired and—"

"I adore your sister. Of course she can come."

He presses his lips together, appearing uncomfortable. I'm not sure why. "Cindy also called."

"I'm thinking about going in at the start of next week," I say, noticing the displeasure on his face.

"She's given you time off, Darcy. Take it."

"I'm not pregnant anymore, Benjamin. Work will be good for me."

I'm surprised he doesn't fight me on it. I wince for him when he stands, imagining the pain. He presses his hand over the wound as he exits the bathroom.

I'm running a brush through my hair when he opens the bedroom door, dressed in jeans and a loose shirt. "She's on her way up."

I set down the brush and run my hand down his back as we make our way out into the living room.

With a ding, the metal doors open, revealing his gorgeous sister.

My heart drops. I force a smile, although I feel as though someone's punched my gut. Her stomach is extended in pregnancy, her maternity dress hugging her body snugly. Her smile is kind when she embraces me tightly. Tears form, and I force myself to look up at the ceiling, praying I can stop.

Dear God, stop, Darcy.

"Thank God you both are okay. I can't believe you didn't call me!"

She hugs Benjamin next, too hard judging by his grunt.

"Did I hurt you?"

He shakes his head, lying. "No, no. I'm just a bit sore."

"You hurt your arm."

"It'll heal in no time."

"Other than that, you are okay? Mom hardly gave me any details."

Of course she didn't. She doesn't know.

"I've have a couple stitches on my stomach, but

that's it."

I shake my head as he gestures her toward the kitchen.

A couple of stitches!

I follow them, glad she's chatty, telling us of her latest trip to Florence as Benjamin reaches into the fridge, pulling out water bottles. He offers me one, but I decline. As much as I want to hide away in the room, I force myself to participate, nodding when needed. As happy as I am to see her again, I can't look at her. I tear my gaze from her stomach and surge out of my chair abruptly, opening the cupboard. I pull out dry pasta, the first thing I see.

"Are you cooking something?" Benjamin is looking at me curiously.

"Yeah, I figured she has to be hungry from the flight over."

"Oh, no. Please, don't wait on me. You're recovering! I'm totally fine."

"I want to. Is fettuccini okay with you?"

"If you're sure…that would be lovely."

I start prepping, aware of Benjamin's strong gaze on my back. I become consumed in what I'm doing, listening into their conversation every so often. She asks me questions now and then, but for the most part, they leave me be, which I'm grateful for.

My heart pumping irregularly, I set the creamy pasta onto plates. Now I have no excuse to move around. When I set the dishes down in front of them, Benjamin's hand is warm on my back, rubbing.

"Thank you, baby. Sit down. I'll get your drink. What will you have?"

"No. You'll hurt yourself," I argue. I pour iced tea into a glass and take a seat next to him.

"So, how's work, Darcy?"

I look up as I push in my chair. "It's fine."

"I heard about your promotion. You're moving up, girl. Soon you'll be as renowned as this one over here." She points to Ben, and he rolls his eyes.

"I don't know about that, but it's definitely the job of a lifetime for me."

"Yeah, I'm taking off a couple of months starting the beginning of August. I don't want any stress before the birth. I read somewhere that exercise is good for the baby, so I've started these morning walks. It's actually refreshing."

I finish off my drink, setting the glass down. It lands with a louder thud than I anticipated. "Really?"

"Becca—"

I hear the wary warning in Benjamin's tone and refuse to look over his way.

"Yeah, I used to *hate* exercising too. I would force myself to do sit-ups in the morning, but other than that, no way. You should definitely try some exercises soon. You're what? Two months Ben said? I can only imagine how excited you must be."

Her hand rubs her extended belly tenderly, loving the child growing within.

I look away from her so fast I hear my neck crack.

I can't. I can't do this.

I shoot up out of my chair in a flash, stuttering through an excuse.

"I...I...my head is hurting. I'm just going to go

take some medicine."

"Okay," Rebecca replies.

Benjamin's eyes are full of concern and knowledge. I lock myself into the guest bathroom and slide down onto the tile.

It shouldn't be this hard. I don't know how I'm going to handle this. How will I see other mothers, children? How will I see them and not be able to imagine what I've lost?

This pain is foreign to me. I've never experienced anything like it before.

I stop breathing and look up from my lap when I hear a hurried whisper come from Benjamin. "Please, Bec, just for now, can you not talk about the baby?"

"What? Why?"

"I should have told you before you even got here." There's a long pause. "We lost the baby in the accident."

We lost the baby.

My lip quivers, and the rest of me threatens to break.

She gasps. "*Oh God*, Ben! And you let me go on like that?"

"I don't know if she wants you to know right now. I feel shitty asking you to tone it down today, but she's going through a lot."

"Oh my God, of course I won't. Why wouldn't she tell me?"

"Darcy is used to handling things on her own. She raised herself, so I think she's so accustomed to dealing with everything on her own she can't let anyone else see the full picture. And then when it overflows and she can't keep anything back, she's completely tormented, completely fucked up."

"Poor girl."

"I haven't even seen her cry about it. I have no idea what to do. I'm so worried I'm going to upset her."

"Ben, I'm sorry. I can't even imagine what you guys are going through. The accident, and then this…"

"I acted like a fucking idiot that day. I was terrible, Rebecca."

"What did you do?"

"I find it hard to even repeat."

"Ben…"

"I-I told her I was only pretending to want the baby so she'd be happy. I told her that." His voice is shaking. "Fuck, Bec, the accident happened literally seconds later. It was like…like I willed her to lose it."

The sound of his wheezing breaths, the low, shocking rumble a man makes when he's trying to stop tears from being shed leaves me frozen, forced to listen to Benjamin break down in front of his sister.

"And when she was crying out in pain, I don't think I was ever so scared. I was sure I was going to lose them both."

"Ben!" she gasps, as if she can't believe it. Knowing their relationship, the last time she's probably seen him vulnerable enough to cry was when Daniel died. "Come here."

"No, I'm fine," he says stubbornly. I'm positive he's pushed her away. "I'm fine. It's all…just a lot."

"Neither of you need to put on a brave face right now, Benjamin. You went through two traumas at once. I know you wanted that baby. This isn't your fault."

"But it is," he cuts her off before she can argue. "Rebecca, it is. I stormed out of that office. I put us in the car. I screamed and upset her."

"Well, when she gets pregnant again, you won't act that way, all right? You both will be careful."

"That means me overlooking the fact that pregnancy could kill her. I don't know how to get right with that. Darcy is my world."

"I know she is," she whispers warmly. "I know. I saw what you were like without her, and I'd never wish that for you again. But she's felt what it's like to be pregnant. That feeling isn't going to just go away, Ben."

"Then we can adopt, you know? Do something else. There's other ways to have a child without putting her in danger."

"That sounds appealing to you, but does it to her? Ben, she just lost a child. I don't know if it's because I've got one growing in me right now, but I find it hard to believe Darcy won't want to try again in the future, and you're just going to have to get right with that."

His silence speaks volumes. She's asking for more than he's willing to give right now. It's crossed my mind multiple times that his grief might stem in some way from the underlying relief he may feel at the loss of the unfamiliar, dangerous territory we were entering.

"I should come back tomorrow," she says, but I've already scrambled to my feet, swiping away any remains of my pain, and opened the door.

I cross the room and set eyes upon them at the table. Benjamin momentarily looks at his lap with discomfort but gathers himself, refusing to let me see what he believes to be weakness. Rebecca smiles, resembling her brother closely as I approach the table.

"I'm sorry," I apologize, and she hops out of her seat, shaking her head.

"No, no. You could have told me, honey. I'm so sorry."

"Don't be," I say, refusing to hold her pregnancy against her. This is a time for celebration for her. I won't be the person to take that away for even a second.

Benjamin remains quiet, assessing me. His words are twirling around in my brain, and because of that, I do my best to keep my gaze from his. I don't want him to know I listened to their conversation.

She gathers her things, glancing at Benjamin. "I will let you guys get some rest. Would it be okay if I stole Darcy from you tomorrow?"

Benjamin gapes, uncomfortably put on the spot. To save him the trouble, I agree, as positively as I can, mostly because I believe another day in seclusion may drive me to madness.

"Good. I'll come pick you up at noon." She hugs me again, this time squeezing just long enough to strike me with emotion and remind me of her pity. I pull back, and she hugs Ben. I scoop up their dishes while he walks her to the elevator.

There's a tight, violent twisting in my chest that began when she entered, but it's lingering like an omen. I'm inhaling fiercely through my nose, trying to catch my breath. My hands are shaking against the white dishes, so I scrub them harder.

It won't always be this hard. I just need to heal.

I can get through this. I've been fine up till now. I've kept it together pretty well.

I slam my eyes shut, exhaling shakily as I see a vision of what I thought she'd look like. Long black hair like her father. Maybe blue eyes like me. A backpack and new sneakers because it's her first day of school…

I'd be quickly throwing together a lunch for her while she eats her Cheerios on Benjamin's lap…

I hear the clatter of the plate falling into the sink as I completely let go, losing hold of myself altogether, the dam finally crumbling. The force of my grief is impressively powerful and steals my air from my lungs. Painful, loud wails come from a deep part of my chest, and I'm unable to hold back. I shield my face with both my hands, gutted by the memories I created in my mind. An arm winds around my chest, and Benjamin's body conforms to my back.

"I-I'm s-sorry. I'm being s-stupid."

"Shh, baby. Shh."

"God, I hate this!" I sob, clutching his arm tightly while he nudges my cheek with soft, tender kisses. He was right. Tonight was my undoing.

"Let it out. Let it out, love."

I suck in desperate gasps, as though I'm running

out of oxygen. He moves his hand from my shoulder upwards, massaging the curve of my neck.

"W-Why does it hurt like this?" I sob. "I can picture her in my head. Why? Why does it hurt like this?"

"Because you already loved her."

His words release a new, powerful wave of tears, and he doesn't let me go. His grip never loosens. Bludgeoning rakes of hurt course through me as I manage to calm myself in his arms. Embarrassed, I reach out for a napkin, hoping removing the tear stains will stop them from falling. My swollen skin resists the rough material.

His phone rings on the table.

"I'm okay. Get it," I say, yearning for a moment alone. He moves slow but eventually does as I ask. He answers his cell briskly, saying only his name.

"No, no. That's the wrong form. We already spoke about this."

His voice fades as he walks away, probably to the bedroom. I set down the napkin on the counter and pick up the plates, determined to finish washing them. The tears don't completely cease.

I shut off the lights and walk into the living room, taking a seat on the sofa. The apartment is dead quiet, other than the soft rumble of Benjamin's voice in the room. My eyes are heavy and ready for the blissful darkness sleep brings.

I don't hear Benjamin when he returns, only noticing when he sits beside me. He lifts the arm not casted, and I gratefully mold my body to his chest, settling into the crook of his arm.

"It kills me to see you like this."

I wish I could wrap my arms around him, but unfortunately, his entire torso is one big battlefield of wounds. I settle on grasping his hand, careful of the healing cut on his palm.

"I wish we could go back, back to our honeymoon…back to when everything was perfect."

He nods his chin against my hair. "Me too."

***

I stand at the dresser staring at myself in the mirror as I chase my medication down with a sip of water. I fondle the strand of black hair I've placed perfectly to cover the couple of stitches I have on my forehead. I honestly have no idea why they look so terrifying, but they do. I run my hand over a yellow bruise on my lip.

Using a dark lipstick, I try my best to cover up what I can. The cons of going out in public. We've been in hiding, and no doubt the media is waiting to catch the first instance we attempt to reacquaint ourselves with the world.

I'm just lucky they don't know about the baby. I press down underneath my eyes, remembering yesterday, remembering the pain. This morning I woke up with no tears. I felt a resolve, a calmness that scares me. I recall what Benjamin said to his sister at the dinner table yesterday.

It's like…like I willed her to lose it.

The words make my mouth dry. The thought that he's holding the miscarriage, the accident, over his head is heartbreaking. Shame falls upon me at the thought that I haven't done much to sway his dark thoughts. I move over to the bed, choosing a pair of black flats to match my dress. With the bathroom door open, I catch a glimpse of my glorious husband.

He has on a clear wrapping around his sprained limb, a clear sling holding up his arm in place. He's running his free hand through his hair, spreading shampoo through the long locks. I'm transfixed by his dominating stance even when completely alone. He glances through the glass, shocked to find me there, watching him. The burns on his chest stand out next to the dark hair trailing over his pecs. His wound, that will most definitely scar, crosses over almost half of his abdomen, looking fierce and painful.

I don't even realize I'm undressing until I open the shower door, stepping in. He's watching me carefully, his hand on his stomach. I'm aware I'm about to ruin all the work I just did making my face look presentable, but I couldn't care less. I shut the glass behind me, now in close proximity with this Adonis of a husband. I raise myself onto my tiptoes, smoothing the shampoo into his hair, making sure all of it is covered. He tilts his head under the shower, letting the water do its work untangling whatever knots there were.

I want to comfort him. I want to adore him and show him love.

"Aren't you late?" he asks.

I drag my fingers through his hair, rinsing out the suds. "Do you know how happy you make me? How good you are to me?"

His spine snaps erect, his face lifting high enough that I can't reach the top of his head. He turns his cheek to me. "Darcy, don't."

"I heard you yesterday."

"I'm sorry." His voice bounces off the walls.

"I won't have you blaming yourself, Benjamin. You got angry that day, yes. You said a lot of things you didn't mean. So did I. We handled all of this so poorly, but that is not the reason I'm not pregnant right now."

He's silent for a really long time, long enough that I've moved on to washing more of him. I caress his arm with soap, careful around the jagged slits where broken glass once covered most of him. He doesn't complain.

"I know you may…you may not believe me, but—"

"You wanted the baby," I say for him, and his silence confirms it. I'm oddly relieved to be speaking openly about this. "I know about the nursery."

His face tilts enough that I can see the uneasy look in his eyes. "You do?"

"Yes, I do." I lift on my toes and kiss the curve of his jaw, where rough stubble has begun to grow. "It's a beautiful gesture."

"I was going to surprise you," he says.

"Which is why I love you…more than anything the world, Benjamin. We both lost a lot that day, but we didn't lose each other. I won't let you hurt yourself over this."

"Everything is so different now. A week ago, our lives were significantly different, and now, we're back…back to what we're used to. Except it's worlds away from that."

"We need to take care of each other, do this together. It's the only way I can stand this."

He nods, slowly, and clasps the back of my neck. "This is forever, Darcy Scott. I'm here."

CHAPTER NINE

Benjamin's sister is a mirror of caution, using our time at lunch to shield me from children, to occupy me with relaying the details of Benjamin's proposal, our marriage. It's admirable how intensely she cares, although I can catch her discomfort whenever someone stares at her stomach for too long or stops by the table to ask how far along she is.

My intimate conversation with Benjamin has made all of this bearable. To enter public society and withstand the intrusive photographs and questions is frightening in itself, but I feel the breaking point has passed. I've gone numb. So when they ask Rebecca about her baby, I find a way to tune it out, to focus on my food or some pedestrian passing by.

It works better than I thought it would.

The chicken salad sandwich I ordered is sitting on the plate untouched. However, I'm on my second glass of freshly brewed iced tea, which this restaurant is known for. I still can't keep much down.

Rebecca regards me kindly after minutes of silence. “It will get better.”

“I know. I know it will.”

My positivity is forced, and it doesn’t slide past her.

“When I heard from Mom that you and Ben were in the hospital after a terrible accident, I don’t think I’ve ever been so scared.”

“Yes, she came to see Benjamin a few days after he regained consciousness, with Alexander.”

Can she hear my disdain?

“Things between them were already rocky with Alexander’s runaround to Ben about parting from Scott Industries. How long did they stay?”

“A few minutes.” I consider whether I should keep my mouth shut and leave their family drama to them. That proves to be too difficult. I set down my glass, sighing. “They asked him for money for their new company.”

Rebecca’s blank stare is a perfect representation of how anyone with a pulse would react to that statement. Alexander had enough grace to look mortified by his mother’s lack of care for her other son, but it didn’t make him rethink taking money from him. That makes them both unworthy in my eyes.

“They did that in the hospital?”

“Yes.”

“How much did they ask for?”

“A million dollars.”

She chokes on her tea. “Excuse me?”

I nod, glad someone is as appalled as I am.

Benjamin acted as if it were an everyday occurrence.

"So they went there and asked him for money and *left*?"

"I reacted to it pretty badly. If your mother didn't completely loathe me before, she does now. I ran after them, told them that Benjamin's heart stopped in that accident, that the doctors had to pump his chest with electricity to revive him. It's a miracle he's here at all."

Rebecca's mouth opens in disbelief. "His heart stopped?"

I glance to my stomach, a flat, hollow thing, a thick lump in my throat. "His sprained wrist? That happened when he shot his arm out to protect me and the baby from the impact of the crash. He was impaled by a shard of glass, and he still found the strength to get me out of the rubble."

Her features have paled considerably, making me believe I've ruined this lunch. But she needs to know this.

"They have no idea how amazing he is. He and I were fighting when it happened, and I know that weighs on him, but he did everything he could to try to help me. They hardly cared, and it destroys me that he knows that."

We're interrupted by the waitress, who deposits our check with the to-go meal I ordered for Benjamin. I take the bill before Rebecca, which is a similar reaction to one Ben gives me when I do that. She doesn't fight me like him though, which I'm grateful for.

"I'm going to give her a piece of my mind

tonight. Alexander too. We have our differences, but we're blood. This shit needs to stop. He's not their bank account."

Her words relieve me a great deal.

"Benjamin would probably kill me for telling you all this."

"You are looking out for him." She smiles. "He's lucky he has someone who wants to fight for him."

***

Benjamin is defying doctor's orders when I enter the apartment, comforted by how well lunch went with his sister. Standing up, bent over his computer, he turns to watch me walk in, speaking to someone low on the phone.

"I won't be back for a few more days, at least."

Not wanting to interrupt him, I approach him only to kiss him. It's a chaste kiss, one that I don't settle on for long. Sex for us is not an option, and in reality, I don't feel the drive for it. My body is weak and slow in recovery. My mind is even worse.

I move to the kitchen, set down his food, and fish a water bottle from the fridge. I'm unscrewing the cap when Benjamin shuts his computer and says, "Tiffany, those tickets I purchased last year…they are still valid, right?" He nods as I regard him suspiciously. "Yes, the London tickets."

I set down the bottle without taking my eyes off of him. What is he doing?

"Can you get us the next flight out? Yes, thank you, Tiffany. Have the tickets ready at the information desk, and inform Dimitri that we are leaving the country."

He hangs up, smiling at how shell-shocked I am.

"*London*?"

He walks around the couches and expensive side tables, approaching me with more grace than he's had for days. He clasps the back of my neck so I'll tilt up to him. I do just that, sure he's insane.

"I always promised I'd take you one day. I think it'd be good for us to…recover a bit. It's perfect timing. Cindy's given you time off. I had no intention of going back for a few more days. Why shouldn't we go?"

I touch his wrist worriedly. He reassures me with a nod.

"Don't concern yourself with that. I'm fine."

I smile, disbelieving. "London?" I repeat, struck stupid.

Benjamin so clearly thrives off of my lack of exploration in the world, wanting to personally introduce me to its wonders. And frankly, I'm tired and in a constant state of uncertainty, my moods fluctuating at the drop of the hat, but his enthusiasm is a plea.

He wouldn't be suggesting this—leaving work, enduring the flight with the wounds he has—if he didn't need it. If he didn't think *we* need it.

We have the luxury of leaving, of taking some time to heal together and focus on something other than our losses, and for that, I will not deny us this chance.

"What do you say?"

I sweep my hands over his silky locks of hair affectionately. "Let's pack."

He lowers his head to kiss me. However, his ever-present phone interrupts us, blaring loudly on the counter. He picks it up and answers.

"Yes, Tiffany?"

The way he blanches, his blood draining under his skin to instantly make him pale and beaten down, when only seconds ago a smile was in place of this frown, scares me shitless.

Whatever Tiffany is telling him has shaken him.

Like an eruption within him, the blood reappears in a boiling rage, leaving him red-faced and shaking. His hand shoots up to his face, which he rubs in disbelief, turning away from me.

"Ben…?"

"Who released that information?"

He storms away, leaving me with only the option to follow. I find him switching on the television, flipping through channels to land on a station.

"I'll handle it. Thank you for informing me."

"What's happened?" I ask when he hangs up. He doesn't need to answer me. He stops on a channel, a news station.

On the screen is the scene of our accident, photographs taken by frazzled bystanders. Benjamin's vehicle as a mangled hunk of metal, molded into a ball. I cover my mouth in horror as they rotate through a group of photos, each one more devastating than the next.

I'm not sure how we lived through that. I'm really not.

I spin around when a shaky recording shows people bent by the crushed window, dragging my limp body out of the smoking rubble. The sight of

Benjamin's arms, still trapped inside, physically sickens me. I have to sit.

"I can't believe this," Benjamin says.

I choke on nothing but air when the reporter mentions our unfortunate miscarriage, the loss of our child, like its breaking news. The lack of privacy is unnerving.

How do they know about the baby?

As if to answer my question, Benjamin's mother appears on the flat screen.

She's all soft words, the epitome of a doting mother who had the scare of her life. She divulges sitting at his bedside with worry, the unimaginable pain at the aspect of losing her daughter-in-law and the baby together. The eyes of the reporter she spoke to lit up and flickered to the camera as she provided the scoop of the century. He makes her confirm that I was truly pregnant, and she gives him the show. A big, disgusting, invasive show.

I simply stare at the events unfolding, only slightly aware of Benjamin's frozen stance a few feet away from me.

Did she do this to spite me?

Does she even have a heart?

Benjamin shuts off the television, already tapping on his cell. He raises the phone to his ear, walking to the window.

"How *dare* you?"

I drop my head in regret and exhaustion. We didn't need this.

"No," he says gruffly, then bellows, "*No!* I don't want your excuses! I don't want to hear another word from you!"

The voice on the other end hums louder, but he talks over it.

"I have things to say, things that are long overdue, and you're damn well going to listen," he seethes, the lines of his back rippling with tension. "You're going to listen because you deserve to hear that you aren't a good mother. You abandoned me after Daniel died."

It's a bomb I'm not prepared to hear him utter. I can't imagine how she's taking it.

He huffs while she talks. I can't make out what she's saying, but it's panicked.

"Neither of you could stand to see my face. You couldn't look at me. I looked so much like him, and you held that against me. I was a fucking *kid*! And to make it worse, in a vain attempt to save whatever was left of your marriage, you adopt another kid when you couldn't even deal with your own. You treated him worse than me, and that is the only reason I give a shit about what happens to him, because he's learned his sliminess from you and from Dad. Bec and I got out of there as fast as we could. We couldn't stand another minute with you."

He pauses to listen to her ramblings. That's what they sound like from here.

"Oh, come on, I know you're not stupid. You knew what you were doing. Don't tell me you didn't know that would get onto the news. That was our personal business that you made known to the goddamn world! I don't care if you don't like her. I honestly couldn't care less what you think about her. She is my wife, and you *will* respect her!

"I've supported you for years! Years! Dad took

the money in the divorce, but that was your fault for being careless and getting caught with that architect. I've paid for everything. Your house, your bills! I was in a damn hospital bed and I agreed to give you a million dollars of money I earned. No more. You're close with Alex now. He can pay for your expenses, as well as that million-dollar loan to start your company. I will not."

He moves the phone away from his ear as she wails. This is twenty-eight years of anger unleashing in one conversation.

"You're wasting your breath." Something she says must stun him. He straightens and growls, literally growls, "What the hell has she ever done to you? She's the best goddamn thing that's ever happened to me. She cares—no, listen to me—she *cares* about me. She cares whether I come home at night, whether I've had a shitty day. She's saved me from living my life like you did. I had no idea how to fucking love! You took that from me, you and my father. I'm done pretending that was okay. Do not expect that check. I would suggest saving the money I've already given you."

Jesus Christ.

He falls quiet, listening.

"Stop crying. You don't mean a single word you're saying. You're afraid because I'm cutting you off." He laughs, near hysterics. "You can tell me you hate me all you want. I don't care. I don't want to hear from you again. Don't call me. Don't call my assistant. You can relay the news to my father as well. I don't suspect he'll care anyway since I haven't heard from him since before the accident."

He flinches at whatever her response was, not completely immune to her venom.

"Always the final say, huh, Mother? Well I'm done. I'm hanging up now."

He throws the phone on the couch and stalks toward the hallway.

I gape stupidly, standing. "Ben—"

He holds up his hand, which is shaking. "Please."

He heads to our bedroom, shutting the door behind him.

***

Benjamin is on a phone call when I enter the bedroom twenty minutes later, doubting that I have given him enough time to digest the separation of him and his parents, but it's not in my nature to retreat or to let him experience this alone.

He hovers by the window, speaking in low tones. At the word *loan*, and *cancellation*, I realize he's talking to a banker. Whether or not he minds that I'm hearing this, he continues, without a glance back. I sit at the edge of the mattress.

"I'm sure. All direct deposits will cease by the end of the week. Whatever she has previously received from me can remain. From now on, I want her off my account."

He's really doing it.

"I'm going out of town, so I'm leaving it to you to see this done. If she contacts the bank, relay to her you've been given strict instructions by me regarding her cease of funds. Yes, thank you for your discretion."

He hangs up and I expect him to speak, then it occurs to me that his mind is so occupied he hasn't realized I'm here.

"Ben?"

My suspicion is correct. He whirls around, showing me the tempestuous storm within his eyes. The chaos clears, and he sucks in a deep inhale.

"How long have you been there?"

"A few minutes."

"Let's start packing."

He crosses the room, removing our luggage from the closet with a grimace.

"You still want to go?"

He flashes me a look of confusion. "Why wouldn't I?"

"*Ben*."

"That woman will not impact my life any further than she already has, Darcy. I'm going to London with my wife."

His tone is not one I'd willingly argue with. I take one of the bags, unzipping it. Benjamin sighs when his phone rings in his pocket.

"It's probably Dimitri wanting the itinerary," he says.

"Go on. I can pack this." I extend my arm and caress the slope of his stubbled jaw, wishing to offer him a moment, just a moment, of understanding.

I don't know much about parenting, having lost mine when I was young. However, I do know about loss and toxicity. It's a hollowness that forms within you, a small, sometimes *big* portion of your body that hollows out in order to let it go, to continue without bitterness.

It's never an easy task and cannot be fixed or filled overnight.

It takes caution, and care, and love to replace what's been lost.

Benjamin's repairing starts in this marriage and under my soft hand.

Neither of us speak, force words that don't need to be said.

He's hurt. I'm sorry for him.

Words won't change that. My touch seems to do the trick.

He holds me there long enough that the phone stops ringing. We share a look, a moment of calm, and then my hand slips from his face so we can carry on.

***

"Please buckle up. We will be beginning our descent in a few moments," the flight attendant whispers to us. First Class is dark and quiet, considering it's the middle of the night. Dimitri is seated opposite us in an aisle seat, wide awake. A book rests in his lap, but he's not reading.

In order to save Benjamin the movement which could impact his wound, I buckle him in and then do mine. We'd been sharing headphones, listening to classical music, which calmed him over the course of the seven-hour flight. The unhinged man who boarded the plane with me is gone, tucked away so his bitterness won't eat him alive.

As his wife, I have the option to try and take his mind off of the stress or have him confront the feelings. I feel I'd be failing him if I allowed him to bury the pain. I don't want to be a person he fronts for. He has enough of those.

"Do you want to talk about it?"

"No."

His shutdown is clear and telling. Well, that's that. With an understanding nod, I turn my gaze to the window, to the endless night. No stars are visible, the sky shrouded with heavy clouds.

"Do you think I'm being cruel?" he asks.

"To her?"

His features, dimmed under the light overhead, only show interest, curiosity to hear my thoughts.

"I'm biased."

"Still. I want to know."

"No, I don't think you're being cruel. Benjamin, ever since I met you, the only time your mother has called has been to ask for something. The only time I saw your father, he had zero faith in the man you know you are…which is a good man. A great man."

His eyes slant disbelievingly. "You're right. You *are* biased."

"I told you." I shrug. "I'm right, though."

"I'm tired of never being enough for her, for them. I could own the world and it still wouldn't make her love me."

His openness is dauntingly transparent, an unheard of action for the infamously collected Benjamin Scott. I don't want it to stop, and keeping an open ear seems like the best option for that.

"I never got to explore. I knew from a young age

how important money was in our world. It infuriates me that they programmed me to be like them, to repel anything resembling human affection. I'm nearly thirty, and I only just learned to want more, with much difficulty and with way too much resistance. I don't blame it all on them, but…"

"I think we are who raises us."

"You're a far cry from the man who raised you."

"He didn't raise me. Without my parents, I raised myself."

"I can't imagine how badly you wish it could have been different."

"I wish they were here, yeah. I wish I hadn't been given to him, of course…but I wouldn't be *here* without all the rest of it. In New York, let alone with you."

He laces his fingers with mine. "You put up with a lot from me."

"Ben, I wouldn't have you be any other way. On the outside, you may resemble them, work like them. On the inside, you are so far from that. You have to know that."

"I do now. The man they raised couldn't love you like I do. It's stronger than anything I've ever known."

***

No sleep on the plane means an entire day is required in bed to recuperate, an unfortunate side-effect of flying—jetlag. The day is gone when we rise to an untouched hotel room, our bags still parked at the door where we left them.

The night is not lost on us though, and instead of trying to sleep while the rest of England does, we ready ourselves for a dinner out on the town. We're poor excuses for twenty-somethings, moving like tortoises over the sidewalk. Dimitri follows behind, alert as ever.

Benjamin is constantly recognized, but Brits have far more reserve than New Yorkers, watching mostly from a distance. I'm sure Dimitri is glad for it. It was only a few weeks ago our faces were plastered on news stations, magazines, social media, survivors of a near-deadly wreck.

London is wet. The ground is scattered with puddles of water after a day of rain. Even now the dark sky looks ready to burst open. Hopefully it won't, since we have no umbrellas. We find a quaint pub with dark lighting and seclude ourselves by the end of the bar, hovering close to each other in order to remain inconspicuous. Although I can't imagine we'd stop traffic halfway across the world, there's honestly no telling.

There's a rowdy group of men a few stools down, occupied with a re-run of a soccer game. Benjamin's medication prevents him from drinking, which would help shake off this unnerving tic that seems to be affecting us both, but he orders me a beer along with wings for both of us. Whether it's just jetlag or something more, perhaps what we've been struggling to overcome for weeks now—the pain of losing someone who would have changed our very foundation in life—I'm not sure, but with this uneasy haze over my emotions, I'm not turning away the chance to dilute them a bit.

What it is about London I don't know. I thought we'd arrive and fall into the same excitement we did in Bali, but we're quiet, both very far away from fun or even escapism.

When Benjamin finally inquires about Kevin, it's confirmed for me. This trip might not be all roses and sunshine. If anything, this foreign place could unload it all.

I embellish Kevin's recent tale of woe, a visit to his mother's with Doug, which he described as a nightmare through fits of laughter. I relay it to Benjamin with just as much enthusiasm until our drinks arrive. Dimitri allows sufficient distance, seated at a table by the window, and won't touch the beer Benjamin has sent over.

It's strange to be together like this. The past weeks have consisted of hospitals and dire situations, stress beyond measure. Lately, the only chance we've had for downtime has been spent trying to reestablish and repair the bond that severed between us the day of the accident.

I think we've forgiven each other for the wrongs committed that day, but just as I can't forget the words he uttered in his anger, he can't forget my betrayal, my failure in trusting him with the conditions I was enduring.

Spotting has stopped, and yet I haven't reached for him at night.

Maybe that's the reason we're so disjointed. Sex has always been a saving grace in our relationship, from the beginning. Through fights, separations, it's brought us back to each other, providing us with a release, an absolution to distance.

He hasn't reached for me either, meaning he hasn't felt healthy enough to or he doesn't feel ready for it. Or perhaps he's unsure whether I'd welcome it. So many questions, with hardly any answers.

The weight of the revelation is heavy and makes me instinctively need to touch him. I place my hand on his back, on the soft cotton material of his t-shirt. Shifting my legs, I twist in my stool to face him, laying my head on his shoulder.

I wonder if Dimitri can tell, if it's noticeable. Dimitri's seen us at rock bottom before. I think we're handling this much better than we did back then.

Even after our food arrives, I find a way to consistently touch him, look at him. Benjamin's phone rings, which he glances at and ignores. In New York, it's just reaching evening. Within a minute, it's going off again, and he sighs.

"It's Tiffany. I should get it."

He dismounts from the stool, exiting the bar to answer the call. I smile at how intently Dimitri watches him from his seat, having been given instructions to stay with me at all times.

The sound of elbows slamming into the counter startles me. "I've definitely seen you around before."

He's one of the men from the rowdy group. Strangely enough, he's American.

"Have you been waiting for my husband to leave so you could come over here?" I ask him, smirking.

"Husband? Damn."

"Yeah, sorry."

"I was hoping he was a boyfriend or even a fiancé. That I could have worked with."

"Oh?"

"When I'm not intoxicated, I'm quite the date. I bring flowers, hold the door open…"

My eyes shift to Dimitri, who has stealthily crossed the room in a matter of seconds and is now seated at the bar beside me. The man is too tipsy to notice. His boys are calling him back over now that the commercials have ended.

"A gentleman, then."

"I mean, yeah. But I can be ungentlemanly if the lady wants it too."

His pass at me doesn't land. He's my age but clearly hasn't come to his own yet. I met so many men just like him working at Marilyn's bar, who tried out the same kind of sleazy lines.

He takes one glance at the diamond on my finger and whistles. "Couldn't give you a ring like that though. How much did that cost?"

Maybe he wants to rob me. He'll have no luck trying with Dimitri breathing down my neck.

"One point five million," Benjamin says, appearing beside him. The man immediately straightens, removing his body from the counter, chuckling at my husband's stealth-like re-entry. Benjamin gestures over to a trigger-happy Dimitri, who has prepared himself for an ordeal. "As our bodyguard would tell you. He helped pick it out."

Benjamin's warning to this poor guy takes a backseat to his admission about the ring on my finger. It's massive, but *holy hell.*

The man is dumb enough to misread Benjamin's

threat. “Holy shit, man. What do you do? Can you get me a job?”

“Maybe if you stop hitting on my wife.”

“All right. All right.” He holds up his hands, smiling guiltily. He gestures to me. “You can’t blame a man for trying. I mean, she’s hot as hell.”

Benjamin places his hands on his shoulders, guiding him away. “Enjoy your game.”

Benjamin reclaims his seat when the man returns to his friends, glaring at how I’m snickering under my breath.

“Oh, you enjoyed that, did you?”

“It’s always nice to be found attractive.”

He clasps the nape of my neck. “Well, if you’re questioning it, then I’m obviously doing something very wrong.”

He says that, and yet he keeps his distance. I don’t remember the last time I kissed my husband—really kissed him. Perhaps it was the morning of the accident, in the throes of passion and lust, just moments after waking.

I don’t question whether my husband finds me attractive. Benjamin looks at me as if I were the last sweet piece of candy in the dish. Starting from the moment I met him, he was gracious and obvious in his desire for me. He made an unsure girl appreciate her reflection, one that had been torn to shreds by a malicious, abusive man. What I question is why does he feel the need to hold back now?

I pick up a wing so I won’t hear Benjamin bemoan my lack of self-regard. Dimitri doesn’t leave my side, doing his best to be invisible to us, but a danger to everyone else.

Benjamin is signing the check when Dimitri hops out of his seat.

"Sir."

Another man from the group has approached and now has the solid wall of Dimitri's hand against his chest, a warning.

"How about you go back to your seat?"

"How about no?" the man snaps back, clearly far more intoxicated than the other one. "My friend told me we're among celebrities. Came over to get a picture."

"As I said," Dimitri forces through his gritted teeth, "you should go back to your seat."

The man is tall, though much thinner than Dimitri or even Benjamin. There's a dark bruise under his eye. He peers at Benjamin, who has a firm hand on my back, urging me up without a word. It's clear the man has been here a while. The smell of liquor is reeling off of him all the way to us.

"We're on vacation. We'd prefer no photographs. Thanks for understanding," Benjamin says, sidestepping to allow me to exit first while Dimitri keeps him away. The group at the other end of the bar, as well as the rest of the dinner guests, have their eyes on us. Mortified at the attention, I keep my head down and move.

"And we'd prefer if you rich snobs gave a shit about working stiffs, but you don't, do you?"

"Connor, man, you're pissed! Leave it alone!"

My hand is grabbed roughly, stopping me in my tracks. I look at the man, who begins to rage about the ring on my finger, and Dimitri has slammed his forearm into the man, Connor, with enough force that his fingers slacken and release me. Just as Dimitri reaches to drag the man away, Benjamin's unharmed arm swings—and lands, his fist connecting with the man's jaw.

I flinch, gaping at Benjamin's outburst. Even Dimitri's eyes widen.

Multiple people stand now, some nervously, others intending to break up whatever fight is about to start. The man, who is stumbling, dizzy from the blow, goes bright red.

I'd be worried for Benjamin if he weren't the same shade.

"You're going to fucking regret that, mate!"

"You picked the wrong day to test me, man," Benjamin snarls, stepping up to him.

"*BOTH OF YOU, OUT OF MY PUB! OUT*!"

"Benjamin, stop!" What's even more confusing is the way Connor's hothead friends begin to hype each other up, actually excited that their friend is about to step into a showdown with a billionaire. All I can think of is the type of press this is going to get if we don't get out of here.

It's gotten so loud between the raging men and the owner shouting that when Benjamin points to Dimitri and then to me, informing him to remain by my side, I hardly realize until he's at the door that he's going out with the man.

"Jesus Christ," Dimitri growls, looking at me.

"You need to stop him. The police…the press…" I say, and he nods, urging me out of the bar with him. The rowdy drunk idiots are slamming into us from behind.

"Benjamin, stop!" I shout upon finding them lost

in some kind of ridiculous rage, toe to toe, landing punches on one another. The man is intoxicated and therefore not at his best. Benjamin is tearing into him with no mercy, so much so that when the man falls onto his back with no intent to get back up, the guys behind us rush around me to get to their friend.

I've seen Benjamin like this before. Again, it was at a bar, when a man laid his hand on me. In many ways, this is just like then. Except even when Dimitri grabs hold of Benjamin from behind, heaving him off the ground to spare the man, Benjamin fights him, too angry to stop.

His shirt has spots of blood on his abdomen, and I gasp, realizing the blood is coming from his stitches.

"You don't know who his father is!" one of the friends shouts at Benjamin, who Dimitri is hauling over to me. "He's going to sue the shit out you, mate!"

Dimitri spins on his heel, pointing at the man. "I know each and every one of your names. Your daddies too. *His*, in particular. I did a background check on every person in that room and had your information at the tips of my fingers from the get-go." He pulls out his phone, dialing a number. I grab Benjamin, who is out of breath, just now coming down in intensity. Dimitri speaks, staring at all the men who look like frightened boys now.

"Hi, Judge Wilkinson? I am the security for Benjamin Scott, owner of Scott—" He chuckles. "Oh, you know? Well, good. Your eldest son, Connor, laid his hands on Mr. Scott's wife in front of multiple witnesses, which can be proven also by video footage from multiple sections of the room. He then instigated Mr. Scott to join him outside to brawl. I'm sure we're on the same page that your son accosted Mr. Scott's wife, and in doing so, Mr. Scott reacted in justified retaliation. Your son will require basic medical attention."

The bloody guy on the ground pales the shade of the sidewalk while his friends surge to their feet, pulling their friend up in the process, as if escaping will help now.

"No, of course, we'd prefer the least amount of publicity on this as well. However, I'm sure people in the bar have begun to spread this…I'm glad we understand each other. If you have any more questions, you can reach me at this number. Goodnight, Judge."

The group is long gone by now, their night put to an abrupt end.

Without another word, Dimitri walks out into the street, holding his arm out to hail a cab. Equally peeved with the impulsive billionaire still regaining his breath, I step off the sidewalk, standing beside Dimitri.

Oh, I've chosen my side.

Dimitri holds open the back door for us before climbing into the front, informing the driver of our destination: the hotel.

"Do you have a first aid kit?" Dimitri asks the oblivious man.

"No, not on me."

"Detour to a drug store then, please."

This is probably the most I've ever heard Dimitri talk. Even when I ask about his life, he answers me in short syllables. Parked at the curb, we wait while Dimitri walks into a store with neon lights and reemerges with a paper bag.

"Hotel, please."

The car ride is silent. Dead silent.

I haven't even looked at Benjamin, mostly because I know he took some blows, and if I see the blood, I'll lose it altogether. Just weeks ago, this man lay on a stretcher, blood coming from him in waterfalls, and instead of backing off, instead of taking the smart way out, he endangered himself and made complications for Dimitri.

I've seen Benjamin's blood far more than I ever should have had to in my life. I'm sick by the sight, brought back to the helplessness of that emergency room.

"Dimitri, I shouldn't have lost it like that," Benjamin apologizes. "I'm sorry."

"I am here for a reason, sir. To protect you from others…and yourself. That man could have been armed."

"He grabbed Darcy. I wasn't going to just—"

"Oh, please. You may have hit him because he touched me. But you pounding his face in? That was for you, Ben. That wasn't in my honor." I meet his eyes briefly with a flash of warning. When he averts his gaze and doesn't fight it, we fall silent again, probably to the disappointment of the driver.

Benjamin takes the bag from Dimitri and hands it over to me when we reach the hotel.

"I'll be up in a moment," Benjamin says.

I leave him with Dimitri, not sure whether he's going to apologize to him again or cover his tracks now that he's calmed down and realized the magnitude of what he's done.

The four-poster bed is re-made, fresh mints on the pillows when I enter the bedroom. After changing into pajamas, removing my makeup, I retrieve the first aid kit from the paper bag and begin pulling items out. I'm hoping he didn't break his stitches or we'll be heading to the hospital.

When everything is in order, I take the time alone to think, holding my heavy head in my hands, shaking at my husband's impulsiveness, his quick temper.

The lock in the door clicks and opens, revealing Benjamin. In the thirty minutes that have passed since the altercation, his adrenaline has surely plummeted, leaving him looking worse for wear. He shuts the door and turns to me.

We stare at each other in silence.

I'm angry and relieved and confused. I want to know what he's feeling, what spurred his violent reaction tonight.

"Come sit down, so I can look you over."

"I'm fine."

"*Sit.*"

He obeys, crossing the room, taking the spot I rise out of. Before his shirt was stained with dirt and blood, it was a smooth, soft cream color. It's one of my favorites and may need to go to the garbage now.

He remains silent while I carefully remove it, leaving him shirtless. Upon close inspection, I'm relieved to see his stitches intact, the blood having dried.

"You're lucky," I say, wetting a cloth. "You don't have to go to the hospital."

"I'm sorry, Darcy."

"I really don't want to hear it right now, Ben. Just let me clean this."

I kneel in front of him, dabbing the area, because even in my anger I'm unwilling to cause him pain. After applying ointment to the affected area, I search for more. The underside of his chin is swelling, which means the guy got at least one good punch in. I crack the ice bag in the first aid kit to initiate the cooling process, and when it's rigid and icy, I hand it to him to place on his chin. I prepare a new bandage to replace the bloodied one, carefully avoiding his gaze.

"We've never really talked about it," I state, pressing the bandage over him, smoothing it out gently.

"About what?"

"About you dying in front of me."

He exhales, reaching for me. "Darcy, I didn't—"

I shake my head, crumpling the wrappers. "You did! Benjamin, you *did*! You were lying in a pool of blood. It was dripping off the stretcher. People were slipping on it. You were completely flatlined."

I see it in my dreams, nightmares every night. Sometimes I wake up in panic, expecting to be in that hospital again, with a different outcome than the one I got.

"They had to sedate me, Benjamin." I breathe with difficulty, wishing he could know, even a little bit, how traumatizing something like that is to witness. I lost a lot that day, but it was so close to everything. It hits now my anger at Benjamin's recklessness isn't even in part to the brawl or his quick temper. I'm angry because he made my pulse leap like it did on that stretcher, leap with fear, and I can't handle it.

"Darcy…"

Already between his legs, I drop the items in my hands so I can lay them upon his skin, having to touch him, kiss him. My lips caress the skin beside the bandage, drifting in soft pecks over his bare stomach.

He stares at me when I take his wrist, the force that then threw me back in my seat in protection. It's no longer wrapped in a cast. I can kiss it without barriers. The bruises on his body are gone now, but I remember where every single one was.

"*Darcy.*"

He pulls me up by my forearms like a child wanting to swing, his grip jarringly tight. Before I can tell him how weak they are, his lips have crushed to mine, sucking the breath from my lungs. I bend to his will, relaxing in submission as soon as I taste him, his tongue, the odd tangy hint of blood from his lip.

This is the kiss we'd been waiting for.

One with the strength of our trauma and love combined as one.

I stretch out, clasping his neck, devoting myself to this joining, swarmed with relief at how firm his mouth is, how he cannot contain his own relief, groaning my name between our brief inhales to catch breath.

"You don't think I've felt that?" he whispers,

tearing away from me. His features are pale and hard, almost with anger at my ignorance. I gaze at him in confusion.

"Your dress was soaking with blood. You were crying, in pain. You kept passing out. By the time I got to you, you weren't even opening your eyes." He cups my face. "It's eating me alive. I can't get past it, this anger, the regret. We had something…something so perfect, and in a second it was gone, replaced by something that could hurt you. And then the possibility was gone altogether and I just…I felt lost. I feel *lost*."

"Perfect?"

No doubt he can see my skepticism, and behind that, infinite hope.

"You didn't begin to dream alone, Darcy."

The rattle. The clothes that are still in the drawer.

By now I'd be showing. My stomach would be beginning to shape. We'd be close to knowing a gender. The baby would be formed enough to know that. Those thoughts are a dark cloud, a parasitic veil that must be released so it won't fester.

"I want to try again, Ben," I whisper, more nervous than I can express to actually utter those words to him. "Maybe not right now, but someday."

His eyes revealed no resistance while also expressing how concerning those words from me are. "The risks…"

"Look at what we've overcome. We've known separation, deceit, heartbreak, grief. Most would have given up a long time ago. We're here, trying. I want a life with you. I want a child that looks like you, acts like you, has your heart. I can do it. I know I can. We just have to try."

Desperation is a tricky thing. Even more, being desperate and aware of said desperation. To ask for something with your whole heart and try to see the decision in their eyes. Is it a yes? A no? If it's yes, is it pity? Is it something years later they'll regret? If it's no, will it ruin us? Will we be able to get past it?

I want Benjamin to want it as much as I do. I want him to accept the risks and go into this with an open mind.

The doorbell rings while I'm searching his expression.

"We don't need to decide anything today." I kiss him softly. "Think on it. We have to both want it."

I scoot from his grasp, bending to retrieve the items I've dropped. The doorbell rings again, and Benjamin rises to get it. I'm not surprised to find Dimitri there.

"The judge wants to meet to insure we won't press charges."

"Where?"

"Hotel bar."

I step into the room and retrieve a clean shirt for Benjamin that buttons down the middle, less of a hassle to put on.

"Downstairs?" he says.

"Yes. He's bringing a lawyer."

"Christ. Superstitious son of a bitch," Benjamin mutters. I hand him the dress shirt. "When?"

"He's already here."

"I'll be out in a minute."

Dimitri exits, and I begin buttoning up Benjamin's shirt while he straightens out the collar.

"I'm sorry I'm leaving like this."

"Don't be. It's fine."

"We'll talk…later?"

He wants to talk more?

He's never been one to encourage it.

I nod, smoothing my hands over the shirt, ridding it of any wrinkles. "I know I don't need to wish you luck."

He leans in, kissing me gently. "I like kissing you. You know that?"

***

My fingers dance along the bed, rattling against the mattress. It's only when I realize I'm alone that I open my eyes, reluctant to meet the light. The sun is rising, brighter due to the clouds that the rays beam around onto London.

A brief search around the room and the lack of warmth in the turned-out covers tell me Benjamin isn't here, but he was. Forcing myself to leave the warmth of the sheets, I move into the bathroom to splash water on my face and brush my teeth. The robe hanging on the door cures the out of bed shivers. The suite outside the bedroom door smells of coffee—fresh coffee.

He's here, somewhere.

His computer is open on the coffee table, along with a notepad and pen.

Noticing it's not the usual work figures and graphs I'm used to seeing, I peek at the tab title, freezing when I notice the M.D. marking. Multiple tabs are still open, medical sites explaining severe cases of anemia, what the causes in pregnancy could be, how to conceive a healthy baby with a chronic disease.

Shell-shocked, I dare to grab the notepad, reading his elegant scribbling…a checklist of necessary precautions, reminders to call a doctor. Tidbits he's taken from real life stories, some hopeful, some frightening.

I wish I could have told him not to look. It only makes it worse.

At the sight of the cracked-open French doors leading out onto the balcony, I suppose I've located him. It groans and squeaks at the same time, alerting him of my presence. In a robe that matches my own, he tilts his head enough to see me.

The sky is painted colorfully. Upon the horizon are yellows and oranges, gradually transforming into a soft baby blue, an indication of a perfect day. His eyes follow me as I step to the edge of the balcony and lean into the brick.

"You're up early."

"Mm, couldn't sleep."

I stretch my arms out along the railing. Despite the dark eyes that indicate lack of sleep, he's magnificent in the new morning light. Dawn compliments him. He's lost weight in the past weeks, which is probably the only reason the robe fits him.

I never tell Benjamin how much I love seeing him right out of bed. The mussed hair, the slimness of his eyes, his taut mouth. He clearly wrapped the robe around himself simply to be presentable around the surrounding balconies. It hangs open halfway down his chest, tied loosely at the waist.

It's too chilly to be out here without it.

"Why are you up?" I ask him.

"I've been remembering."

"Remembering what?"

"A lot. What my life was like a few years ago."

"When you were the king of bachelors?"

He smirks. "That's an interesting way to put it."

"It's the truth, isn't it?"

He nods. "I keep thinking of that day, the one you brought up when you told me you were pregnant."

"The night we first slept together."

"Yeah."

"What about it?"

"I went into that bed expecting to come out of it with some pleasure, an inevitable release of the strange hold you had on me until that point. Instead, I came out of it blind in love." He shakes his head. "I told you that I didn't love you then, when we fought over the baby, but I'm realizing that's not even true. I did."

"I…didn't know that."

"You were just someone, a beautiful woman who could hold her own and wouldn't take my shit. I liked that about you. But it was the marks, the scars along your back, and your hesitance to show them to me that made it impossible to compare you to any of the others."

I'm rosy pink by the compliments, by his candor. I tilt my head, wondering why he's telling me this.

Sensing the chill that runs through me, he holds out his arm for me to join him.

"The stitches…" I remind him.

He makes a face. "Oh, come on. They're fine."

I lower onto him, lifting my knees to find a comfortable place on his lap. He offers his coffee mug to me. The steamy ceramic feels great against my cold hands.

"Is there anything you miss? Of that time?"

"My doorman would wake me then, Darcy." He kisses my shoulder, pushing back my hair. "To calls, and figures, and business. Now I get a smile. Blue eyes. These hands. A warm body to invite me near. I don't miss a damn thing."

Christ, I can't take him being this agreeable, this affectionate, this early in the morning. It's going to send me into overdrive. I set down the coffee mug on a small patio table and find better use for my hands—buried in his hair.

"You're my husband," I point out simply.

That time he's talking about, I couldn't even dream of uttering those words to him. He would have fled into the night at the mere thought. Benjamin's eyes now don't even falter in the slightest at the mention.

He traces the line of my throat lightly. "You're my wife."

"You'll never have to be that man again."

He nods. "No. A husband, yes. A father…"

My heart begins to slow, its beats strengthening with anticipation and hope. "A father? Wait, what are you saying?"

"I'm saying…no more birth control. No more

condoms." He clasps my face, searching my bewildered expression. "I'm saying we throw out caution and see what happens."

Holy shit.

"You want that?"

"It will be hard. I will not go easy on you. Your safety will matter above all."

I nod, finding it hard not to beam from ear to ear. It's hard to believe. "You really mean it? You want this?"

"Yes."

My mouth hangs open in disbelief. "*Benjamin…*"

"You'll need to bear with me. My fears haven't dissipated overnight. I have no rulebook to go by."

"We'll make our own."

"I've prided myself on being able to give you the world. I refuse to deny you the only thing you've ever asked for."

An unspoken promise in the air hangs the longer we're still, embedding the decision deep into our marrow. I'm unsure as to his thoughts, other than what he's showing me. True to the man I fell for, his eyes show mostly decision, a resolution that he's found a way to understand and accept.

My thoughts are on the secret moments he shared with his sister when he thought I was out of earshot. The confessions he spoke to her, his reluctance to attempt to conceive again. Remembering the way he broke down beside her reminds me how monumental this change of heart, or rather change of mind, is.

He holds me like I were the world.

He's injured; my body is weak.

It doesn't matter.

"Come to bed with me," he whispers.

When I roll onto the tips of my toes, extending my arm for him, I've given my answer. We enter the luxurious suite, deciding a path of life.

We disrobe on our way into the bedroom. When we clear the door and I'm twisting, a nervous pit in my belly, I'm captured by hands that grasp me like they lack the ability to let go.

There's nothing in his movements, in the noises he makes, that suggest he's rethinking anything. Our usual push and pull is present, and when he brings me onto the bed, careful of our current fragility, I hardly recall the feeling I had that made me not want this.

His weight settles onto me, the pressure sinking me into the mattress, and my air is gone. He's going to take this slow. I can see it in his eyes, feel it in his caresses.

This is a moment we make as adults. As people who see a future and chase it.

In this moment, we're not only married. We're partners, on the same wavelength.

As he sinks into me, both of us aware we lack protection, I vow silently to do my best. I vow to give him a child, to give him the life he was denied.

Our children will never know poverty, something I know a great deal about. But they will be abundant in love…something we both lack experience with. It will heal us in a way nothing can, I'm sure of it.

And I vow that I will love them both from the

depths of my soul.

Lost in London, as the sun rises over the surfaces of the bedroom, we pledge life to one another, setting a steady course.

***

Benjamin's smile widens as I pore over the plaque inside of Jane Austen's home, my favorite author, glancing at him to see if he's making fun of my enthusiasm. He purchased a gift for me two Christmases ago, before our lives fell into disrepair, my favorite novel by her. I'm soaking in the chance we've gotten to explore my heroine's home.

I feel the majesty here. It's a bibliophile's dream.

There's a steady flow of visitors, quiet people who marvel as much as I do. Benjamin stands out like a sore thumb, holding my jacket over his forearm…Dimitri even more so. Mostly women are in the room, none of whom can tear their eyes off my husband, who could have fallen right out of one of Austen's novels.

I don't blame them for staring.

"I can't believe I'm here. I can't believe *she* was here. She wrote *Sense and Sensibility, Pride and Prejudice* here. Masterpieces," I muse, extending my arms to accentuate the gravity of the situation.

"Your Mr. Darcy." Benjamin hums and then twists in place, extending his hand out to Dimitri, a cue for something. Peeking around the looming frame of my husband, I catch Dimitri's hand disappear into his thick coat. He pulls out a book.

He hands Benjamin my copy of *Pride and*

Prejudice, the first edition he purchased for me years ago when our future seemed so uncertain. He sets the hardcover into my palms.

"Now you can set it down. A first edition, right here where she wrote it."

A number of women who were eavesdropping make loud, disbelieving noises at my husband's words. They come up beside me, asking to see the copy, worshipping the man before me like Mr. Darcy himself.

I bask in my pride to be married to such a man, who tells Dimitri to remain calm despite the swarming women.

"You are a lucky woman."

"The *luckiest*."

When asked, I show them the printer's date, the proof of edition, and they collectively attach themselves to my splendor.

"Well, do what he says," one of them says, grinning. "Set it down."

We go silent, like true faithful fans, staring at the object like it will levitate any minute. This goes way past bucket list dreams.

After a few seconds, we disperse to allow others into the room. Hearing the women's goodbyes, I take the book and spin into Benjamin, laughing, hopping with glee.

I tighten my arms around his neck, more grateful than I can say. "Thank you, Benjamin."

CHAPTER TEN

New York is famous for diners. Greasy, dirty diners.

It's a rare day when I can get Benjamin to enter one. However, today is an important day. We've pulled three tables together to accommodate the guests. Benjamin suggested somewhere nicer, but Kevin insisted on this place, swearing it had some special power.

It was the place Doug and he came to after the club the night they met.

On Doug's hand rests a gold ring—an engagement band, one Kevin just put on him in Central Park, before bringing him to this place to celebrate with his friends and family. Some people I know, like Kevin's parents. Some I don't. Marilyn, my eccentric friend, hasn't changed and has brought along a date none of us have met before. Beside Kevin sits Doris, who is admiring the lovely sight of a table full of smiles.

I've been doing the same thing.

Benjamin is talking to Kevin, informing him of

venues, insisting on paying for whatever they can't afford. Knowing Benjamin, I'm sure he fully intends to pay for the entire wedding. Kevin is both appalled and touched, as am I. Everyone is talking over each other, and no one gets tired of it.

Kevin is still arguing when Benjamin pierces me with his soft green eyes. "Get your friend to agree, all right? Help me here."

"It's crazy! A wedding costs a fortune!"

Kevin's father, a man who is Latin to the bone, sticks out his chin pointedly toward Benjamin. "The family must pay for the wedding. No exceptions."

They don't have the money. I know it, Benjamin knows it, and Kevin knows it.

Benjamin holds up his hands, a true negotiator. "All right. I can respect that. However, there's no problem with us paying for the reception. It could be a wedding gift, right, Darcy?"

I smile secretively, shrugging my shoulders to my best friend, who is looking upon us both in shock. "I don't think he's going to take no for an answer."

Kevin glances at his father, who is squinting at my husband. "Dad?"

Salvador nods, wagging his index finger at Benjamin. "I pay the wedding. You do the reception."

"Done," Benjamin says triumphantly, finally leaning back in his seat.

Doug is just as bewildered as me and everyone else at the table.

"Did that just happen?" Kevin asks, beaming ear to ear. He looks between us. "Thank you both. I really don't know what to say."

"It's Benjamin," I laugh. Everyone at this table knows damn well I'm not the one making millions.

"It's from *both* of us. You've always been a great friend to Darcy."

Doris leans toward the lovers, wanting to hear more about the sunset proposal.

Benjamin turns his attention to me, chastising without malice. "We talked about this. We agreed—"

"Yes, but I'm contributing little here, let's be honest." He lifts my hand, pressing his mouth to my diamond and the wedding band.

"What's mine is yours, Darcy."

"Benjamin!" Marilyn exclaims, waving to get his attention from the other side of the table. "Come over here! I want you to meet someone!"

I smirk, leaning close. "She thinks her boyfriend of the month will be an asset to Scott Industries."

Thankfully, he looks amused, setting down his napkin. "Is he?"

"He's only ever been an intern."

Benjamin laughs, rising to his feet. "Wonderful."

I watch him go to appease my friend, admiring the way they look at him. It's taken years, but in that time, he's gained their respect. They expect, and like, when we're together.

It's been six months since London. Six months of taking pregnancy tests, of getting my health back in order. Each month has been a negative, and I convinced myself it's my health.

Once it's regulated, then the chance will come.

We will succeed.

It's hard to dwell on the lack of the addition we're trying to achieve when for the first time, we're leading a completely normal life. Well…normal for us. We're working. We're laughing, fucking, and fighting—we wouldn't be us without that.

We're constant newlyweds.

Doris sits down in Benjamin's vacant chair, tearing me out of my reflections. She squeezes my hand.

"I read recently that if you do the deed on a full moon—"

To spare us both the uncomfortable aftermath of pregnancy superstitions, I stop her, shaking my head. "Oh, please no."

"It's just something I read. I might work."

I'm the shade of a fire hydrant. "I'll keep it in mind. We're really just taking it slow. There's no rush."

"You saw the doctor yesterday, right?"

"Yes. My health is better, which is worrisome because it definitely means it's pregnancy that starts the decline. They thought it was a sickle cell trait at first since my father was of Italian descent, but the test came back negative. They have no explanation why my immune system was struggling so much."

"There has to be something they know."

"She mentioned that I might have an incompetent uterus, which would weaken me in pregnancy, but it doesn't explain the loss of blood cells. She just mentioned the risks again, that we'd have to take this as cautiously as possible if we truly want children. Any outcome is possible."

"I don't like this talk," she sighs, refusing to hear it. "You're fine. You'll be fine."

"I know I will," I say. "It's not me that needs convincing."

Her eyes gravitate to my husband, who is deep in conversation with Marilyn, a woman who has adored him from the start. She was always pulling for us.

"How is he handling all this inconsistency?"

"He absorbs it mostly, doesn't say much, but I can see it scares him when he thinks about it too much."

"Benjamin with a baby…that would be quite a sight, wouldn't it?"

I long to see that sight. I lose myself in his movements, his smile. "Mmm."

"It feels like just yesterday I was interviewing you for the position."

The flashbacks that hit me are cringeworthy. "I fell over myself when I laid eyes on him. I was a goner. Been so ever since."

"For him too. He's married now, trying for kids. God, there was a time if I had heard myself saying that, I would have thought I'd started to lose my marbles. It's amazing what a good woman can do for a lost man."

"And what a good marriage can do for two lost people," I add, unable to look away from him.

***

Good sex is therapeutic. *Great* sex is straight healing.

A lot of it and your nerves are sensitive, your mind is awake, senses heightened.

It's mid-day, smack dab in the middle of a work week. Benjamin's briefcase is on the floor by the door, having fallen off the side table in the process of the hasty removal of his clothing. Articles of his suit are scattered across the floor, my dress and lingerie mixed in the mess of dark colors.

Snow is falling fast outside the window in an almost horizontal downpour, the last of winter coming down with all its might. It's almost below freezing outside, but we're unable to feel any of the chill.

His hands are like fire, his fingertips scalding hot as he traces them over my body. We're facing each other on the massive mattress, tangled limbs in the middle. His cock is inside of me, as it has been for a good portion of this snow day we've taken for ourselves.

His palm urges my ass into him, pushing and pulling me in slow, unrhythmic movements. No gracefulness, no urgency. We're fucking simply to be within each other. My hands scale his damp skin, up into his hair, the dark wet spirals at the end that are so comforting to grab on to.

For the fifth time, his phone blares, a distant call from the living room where he left it.

And for fifth time, it goes straight to voicemail.

His lips are pushing into mine, his tongue driving between them, curling and sucking me in. It's enough to make someone incoherent. My thigh is wrapped around his waist, my chest up against his chest. When his touch trails from my backside, taking the slope of my spine to my neck, which he grasps tight enough to keep me in place, ultimate protection sweeps through my skin, my blood, and bones.

Every part of me is here.

We're getting there without a single utterance. No dirty talk, no urging. We're hardly moaning now, lacking enough breath to do so. The end is within reach, but he slows us down, forcing us to wait together.

It's so close my fingers are contracting violently over him, my stomach tightening from the build up. I let it go, smiling against him.

My husband wants to make it last. I cherish that gift.

***

A plus sign.

Such a small, insignificant symbol…for anyone but an expectant woman.

Kevin is waiting outside of the door of the drugstore, mostly impatient. "That thing's gotta have worked by now, right?"

The pregnancy stick is on the sink, and both of my hands are clasping onto the sides for dear life. When I noticed I was a week late, I decided I'd wait one more before running out to purchase a test. Somehow, I convinced myself it was too soon to know. I convinced myself I was jumping to conclusions, only hurting myself in the process. We've had months and months of negatives, and yet, here it is.

That little pink plus sign.

"Darcy, what does it say?"

"I'm pregnant," I whisper, although there is no possible way he can hear it.

"What?"

Thick tears are dropping from my eyes into the sink. I'm struggling for breath as joy takes me into its arms. I snatch up the stick and whirl around, unlocking the door. He does the rest of the work, throwing it open.

I hold it up, my mouth hung open, my cheeks wet. "I'm pregnant."

He stares at the stick in my hand, and then his features become more like mine. "No fucking way."

"I'm pregnant," I repeat, my voice on the edge of madness, complete deliriousness.

"Holy shit!"

Kevin wraps his arms around me in a chokehold, lifting me off the floor with a shriek. He sets me down abruptly, completely unaware of the looks we're getting from shoppers.

"It can't be real," I gasp.

He shakes me, grinning. "I'm getting another one. Maybe two. We'll make sure before you tell him, all right?" He kisses my cheek exuberantly and rushes into an aisle to snatch up two more pregnancy boxes.

Before you tell him…

***

"Hi, Tiffany." Benjamin's assistant has already been informed of my arrival and is waiting outside of her office.

"Darcy, hello. He's about to get out of a meeting any minute."

"No rush." I wonder if she can see how badly my hands are shaking.

My heart is on the outside of my body. I'm wearing it like a damn brooch.

"Can I get you tea? Coffee? Anything?"

"No, I'm okay."

"You sure? It's real cold out there." She nods decisively. "I'll get you a tea."

Knowing she won't take no for an answer, I take a seat in the chic waiting area. She reappears with a steaming mug and, after a few more polite words, disappears back in her office where no doubt a pile of paperwork rests.

I sip the tea, my stomach flopping and turning with nervousness. How will he take it?

Will he be excited? Will he not react? Will he hide his true reaction?

I'm pregnant. I have a baby growing inside of me.

The chaos is just around the corner, I can feel it. The worry. The excitement. The anticipation.

The door to Benjamin's office opens, a hand flat against the glass to keep it ajar. The shiny watch on Benjamin's wrist tells me it's him as men pour out of the room, laughing. They know who I am by now, and although I can't recall any of their names, they greet me warmly as they pass to make a good impression on the boss's wife.

"Darce?"

I glance at Benjamin standing in the doorway of

his office, a curious look on his face.

"Did I miss an appointment? Dinner?"

I shake my head, picking up the mug from the coffee table and walk past him into his spacious office.

"Are you okay?" he asks.

His desk phone rings, and he reaches across, slamming it down to end the blasted blaring.

"I'm…better than okay." I lift my chin.

Bent over his desk, he glances at me, piecing together my sudden appearance. In so many ways, this mirrors the first time I came here to divulge the same news to him.

Except this time, he reacts.

"You're…?"

I nod. "Yes."

I see so much in such a short amount of time. Disbelief. Awe. Confusion. Realization. Excitement. And then…blistering happiness.

He rushes over to me, capturing me in an embrace. "You're pregnant," he breathes, wanting the confirmation.

I can't keep the smile from my face. The tears are back with a vengeance, rolling down my cheeks. "I'm pregnant. I-I checked three times. I'm—"

His lips slam into mine, and he lifts me up, stopping me from saying more. I wrap my long legs around his waist.

I'm on clouds. I'm in the stratosphere.

He's happy.

He's actually *happy*.

Benjamin sets me down onto his desk, pulling back with a breathless gasp. I stare at him, full of every possible emotion as he sweeps his thumbs over my cheeks, looking lost for words himself.

I laugh softly, taking his hands, which show how overcome he is.

"They're shaking," he whispers, his face flushing with embarrassment.

"Mine haven't stopped either."

He brings my hands to his lips, kissing my knuckles tenderly. I watch him closely, not wishing to miss a single moment of this. It wasn't even a year ago this same news was met with panic and resistance…disdain even.

I underestimate his ability to adapt more than I should. From the beginning, he's proven time and time again that he's capable of change, of growth.

There's no telling what is in store. The trials and tribulations we'll have to endure.

But now more than ever it's clear we're doing this together.

He pulls me close, letting me surrender to his warmth, and I mold to him naturally, tucking my face under his chin, seeking only his understanding, his strength to encourage my own.

"I think we're ready now," I tell him, reminded of our uncertain days before.

His heartbeat is a steady drum in my ear. "I think we are."

***

My gaze is on the New York skyline. At the edge of the balcony, I reflect, as I have always done in this place. It could be the breeze that blows this high in the air that makes the hot summer air less damp. The seasons are moving, and time is unstoppable, passing with our excitement.

My belly is against the railing, a gigantic force beneath my breasts.

The first few months were met with excitement, an unnatural, consuming excitement. It wasn't hard for that to turn into worry at the first sign of trouble. We knew my health would decline. We knew tests would need to be run, precautions taken. We knew better than to tell anyone about the baby until I'd begun to show.

By the fifth month, when my stomach really popped, we found a common ground between the two emotions. I'm well aware this may be the only time I carry a child, as I have no idea what lies ahead, what birth will do to my body.

I've found the ability to bask in it, without letting fear overrule me. With medications, supplements, and leave from my job which pretty much confines me to the apartment, I make it work.

I can handle fatigue. I can handle nausea.

If the outcome is a healthy, happy baby with Benjamin's eyes, I can do anything.

My fingers glide over the railing. I can close my eyes and see a different time. A time where I stood right here, so ridden with fear and rage that I left Benjamin. How terrified I was for that trial, for the prison sentence I was nervous I'd receive for defending myself against a sick man. I changed with that sentence and lost myself. And as I changed, so did Benjamin, who suffered along with me in the dark.

He knew before I did what we needed in order to restart…to bind to each other forever.

My recollections have disturbed my mind and, therefore, the little one inside of me. I press my hand to my belly, rubbing the soft cotton of my dress. I'm not sure if it's the infamous "nesting phase" that brings on these torrents of emotions, but they're hard to get a handle on.

I wipe my cheeks, refusing to go there tonight. Benjamin comes back from his trip today. For the first time since we married, he had to travel overseas, which I had no clearance from the doctor to do. Four days are a lifetime when you have nothing to do but sit and stare at a wall, watching time tick by. It was comforting how hard he tried to put off going to Taiwan, but in the end, it couldn't be helped.

Nine more weeks and there will be another here with us, a sweet baby to keep me company.

"*Wife*."

I smile at the sound of his voice, pursing my lips to the sunset.

"Husband."

He's just outside the sliding door. He's shed his suit jacket, and his luggage, but still stuns in a three-piece vested suit. He crosses the small amount of space it takes to reach me and takes my mouth without delay, catching the back of my head with his palm to limit his force.

His eyes are warm when he pulls back, like my mouth has drugged him. They sweep over my body eagerly, and I admire the way his lips curve appreciatively.

"Everything good?"

"Yes, everything's been fine here. Your trip?"

"In and out, easy. Wish I could have come back sooner."

"Back to uneventfulness?" I chuckle. "You were traveling in Taiwan amongst beautiful things…beautiful people. Fun people who can do things. I mean—"

"You're becoming green," he says in amusement. I roll my eyes, turning on my heel. He catches me from behind and pulls me to him, placing his chin on my shoulder, his lips on my neck. "My people are right here."

He cradles my belly, sending an instant jolt to my heart.

"Besides, you being uneventful has its advantages," he continues, his voice warming with playfulness. "You have nowhere to be."

Another great perk of the nesting stage: constant insatiability.

I shiver at the mere implications.

"And you don't either?"

"Nope."

I grin. "What advantages?"

"Come inside and I'll show you."

***

"It's the wrong blue."

Sitting on the plastic-covered rocking chair, I show Benjamin the blue on the paint barrel, which prompts him to check over his own paint mark. He makes a face, shoving the roller to the wall.

"It's navy blue."

Kevin enters the room with a tray carrying beer for them and lemonade for me. My dear friend clucks his tongue in distaste at the uncomfortably dark blue on the wall of the nursery. This was once Benjamin's piano room, the instrument which now resides in the living room.

"That color is too dark for a baby room."

"It's depressing," I add.

Benjamin rolls his eyes, taking the beer from Kevin. "It's the color from the catalog."

"It *so* isn't," Kevin argues, bending to retrieve the evidence. "See? They must have sent the wrong one."

I stand up, which has recently become increasingly difficult, and Benjamin looks pointedly at Kevin, who is supposed to be forcing me to rest while he works.

"What do you think you're doing?"

I hum cheekily. "I didn't put on these overalls for nothing."

Benjamin frowns. "Kevin, you are utterly useless."

"What? She's *your* wife," Kevin counters, taking a long drag from his beer.

"John and Jasmine are coming later to help, and they will think I'm running you into the ground if they find you up like this," Benjamin says, refusing to give me his roller.

Laughing, I reach for it then have an evil idea.

I grimace and drop my hand, clasping my belly, and Benjamin stills.

"Baby?"

I reach out and snatch the paint roller from his hand while his guard is down and grin when Kevin gasps at my sneaking abilities. Benjamin's face tightens, and both Kevin and I get a good laugh from my husband's shock. Finally, I relent, feeling bad.

"Okay, I'm sorry. I'm sorry."

"That was a shitty move," Benjamin mutters, too relieved to be pissed.

"I'm not going to keel over painting a damn wall, all right? Watch and learn."

I pour the rest of the white paint primer into the tin of the dark blue, using the roller to mix them together. When it's a pretty light blue, I straighten with a hand on my aching back.

I'm due in a week, and I'm beginning to feel it.

"See? Problem solved."

"All right, smart ass. Sit down," Benjamin says, gesturing to the chair.

"I want to paint."

"Tough."

I waddle over and stop in front of him, stubbornly meeting his eyes, which are equally stubborn.

"Oh, my love, you're going to get *nowhere* with that scowl."

I stretch up onto my toes, turning so my stomach won't hit him, and clasp the back of his neck, planting my lips onto his.

"Get a room!" Kevin yells.

Benjamin submits easily to my mouth, his lips shaping into a smile against mine.

When he pulls back, I look down where I've

placed the roller between us.

"Oh, that's great. That's real great," he says while I continue to mark him with sky blue paint, now getting his arm. "I'm going to have to change now."

I move back, observing my handiwork. One look at Kevin and I'm convinced my husband has never looked hotter. The white t-shirt, denim pants spotted with paint look is definitely one he should utilize more often. Kevin blows out a breath of desire and averts his eyes to remain faithful to his fiancé. I don't have to have such restraint.

"This is actually quite a look for you."

"Oh, you like it, do you?"

"Mmm."

I head for the wall, and he makes a sound. "Darcy."

"I'm fine, really. I feel great."

The chime of the elevator dings from the corridor.

"That will be John and Jasmine," Benjamin says, wiping his hands on his jeans. As soon as he's gone to retrieve them, Kevin comes to stand by me.

"Did you see? He went white when you joked with him like that. I can't wait to see what he's like when it's the real thing."

***

"Darling, I refuse to give you caffeine of any sort, no matter how badly you want it, so I brought you—"

Doris stops in her tracks at the sight of me. I'm

standing in the living room, water dripping down my thighs and onto the puddle on the floor. *My Best Friend's Wedding* has just started on TV, but my body has other plans for today.

Today, we make a baby.

Before I start hyperventilating, Doris is on the move, dropping the mugs onto the table with enough force that the hot chocolate splashes onto the surface. For an older woman, she moves nimbly, rushing to the phone to alert Dimitri, who has been on stand-by for days, that he needs to get up here. By the time he's exiting the elevator, Doris has my hospital bag on her shoulder and is walking me over to him.

I'm moving fast, knowing contractions are on their way.

"It's happening," I tell Dimitri nervously when we board the elevator. He smiles kindly, already knowing what my next words will be.

"I called Benjamin. He was on his way out of his office before we got off the phone."

"Good."

"You're going to have a baby!" Doris cries, wrapping her arms around me. I'm too frightened to hug her back, feeling movement within me, a sharp tightening, growing in intensity. Right when we exit the elevator into the lobby, I'm hit by the first contraction, which honestly feels stronger than I thought it should.

I keel over, blowing out a breath, grimacing at the uncomfortable cramping in my stomach. "I don't like this. Ooh, I don't like it."

"Just breathe through it. Breathe and it will

pass."

"Just think, when we reach the hospital, they can give you drugs," Dimitri says.

I look at him, shocked enough at his statement that I manage to laugh. "I told them I didn't want drugs. They…advised against it due to my condition," I admit.

"Oh, well…you may want to rethink that."

***

"*Fuck*!"

I tighten my fingers around the side of the bed as I stand, momentarily blinded from the contractions that are now only minutes apart. Doris is rubbing my back, cooing to me softly, reminding me to breathe through it. By the time I made it to the hospital, my contractions were too close. Drugs are now a distant dream.

"Find out where Benjamin is," I plead breathlessly as soon as it subsides.

"Okay, honey. Okay."

She opens the door as Dimitri is coming in. He is probably whiter than me.

"Where is he?"

"In traffic. Construction blocked off the intersection."

"Fuck," I groan. "How far?"

"I'm not sure. He…was running when we got off the phone."

Both Doris and I look toward the window, uttering the same thing at the same time. "It's raining."

I momentarily become calm enough to picture my husband, Benjamin Scott, racing through vehicles in a storm in order to make it to the birth of his child.

"Oh, Christ." I feel another one coming on. "They're real close now."

Doctor Trigiani enters the room, followed by another nurse. I'm punched in the stomach, slammed by another contraction.

"How far apart are they?" she asks the nurse.

"Minutes now."

"And the husband?"

"On his way," Doris says. I deflate into the bed, my legs wobbling when it subsides, and Doctor Trigiani wastes no time getting me onto the bed to check my cervix.

She places her hand on my leg reassuringly. "Okay, Darcy, it's time."

I shake my head, glancing at the door. "N-No, he has to be here."

"This baby is waiting for no one, honey. It's time to push."

"It's okay, Darcy," Doris says, rubbing my hand with her gloved one. I stare at her, wild with exhaustion as the professionals prepare the tray, and the table, helping place my legs into stirrups. "He'll be here soon."

***

The volume of my wails far exceed Doctor Trigiani's orders, which she must bark out in order to retain my attention. My head is heavy, my chin pressed into my chest as I push, feeling as though unconsciousness is only a few seconds away. I drop my head back to breathe when there's a commotion at the door.

Tears spring to my eyes and I blubber at the sight of Benjamin in his suit, drenched head to toe. Someone comes to force him to leave, and I panic.

"No! What are they—"

"Focus, Darcy. Focus. Another contraction is coming."

"He has to change before he comes in," Doris says comfortingly in my ear, calm as hell. "It's procedure."

"I need him here!" I sob, losing hold of myself altogether. "I need him—"

I crush Doris's fingers, gritting my teeth enough to hurt when the doctor's warnings hit me full swing, stealing the breath from my lungs.

I don't know how anyone can bear this.

I want to force them to give me the drug. I *need* the damn drug.

"Oh god! Oh god! It hurts!"

I moan, tasting my tears. Doris's fingers slip from my grasp, and someone else's replace them. Benjamin is suddenly right there, right next to me, inches away from my face. There's no fear in his eyes. I can't imagine how much is in mine.

In no control of my emotions, I sob loudly, relieved when he pushes the wet hair from my face, whispering to me.

"I'm here, baby. It's going to be okay."

"I'm scared, Ben," I tell him, my body pulsing with pain. "I'm being torn in two. I wasn't before, but I am now. I-I…don't know if I have it in me."

"We're at the finish line, baby. You're almost there. He's almost here."

I close my eyes, my body warning me of more.

"We're close, Darcy. You're beginning to crown," the doctor says. "I need you to push big here. Push!"

I do as she says, and my growl of pain crescendos into a war-cry kind of bellow.

"The head is out!"

I sigh with relief and drop my head back. Benjamin laughs nervously, kissing my cheek. "Breathe, Darce. You're almost there."

"Push! Push!"

I'm blind. Everything is a static, gray, blurry mess.

A tiny infant's wail fills the room, the pain having reached its peak. I'm on the decline now. I sink into the mattress in sheer exhaustion.

"Oh my god," Benjamin says in awe, kissing my flushed skin tenderly. "You did it. Holy shit, baby."

It's when I try to laugh and nothing comes out that I begin to sense something is wrong.

"Darcy?"

I hear the change in his tone, a slight hint of fear in his voice. Suddenly, Doctor Trigiani's speaking over him, ordering the nurse, "Get him out of the room."

"What? What's happening?"

"Your wife has lost a lot of blood. She is under duress, Mr. Scott. I need you out, *now*."

"Darcy?"

His voice is only fear now. I can't open my eyes

anymore. I'm tired.

I can't hear the baby anymore. My baby.

"*Darcy*!"

***

A steady sound of a pulse echoes through my ears.

Coming to my senses, I attempt to wiggle my fingers, flicker my eyelashes, and am rewarded with a hint of light. Almost instantly hands are caressing my face, soft and gentle.

"Baby…"

I part my eyelids reluctantly, facing the blinding white light.

I need to see him.

Benjamin eyes are piercing green, red-rimmed and glossy by his emotions. I blink at him slowly, sucking in short breaths. The monitor begins to beep faster as I remember what took me under.

"Ben…"

I'm not sure whether it's the race he made to get to me in time, the stress of the delivery, or the fear he endured when I began hemorrhaging, but something overcomes him. He drops his head onto my chest and loses himself altogether. Not gentle hiccups. No. He's sobbing enough to shake me.

I lift my hands groggily and glide them into his hair, holding him to me.

"It's okay," I croak, my throat parched. "I'm okay."

"Oh god, Darcy," he groans, pulling himself up ungracefully. He's still in the same teal scrubs as before. He wipes his tears and bites down on his lip to gather himself. "I…fuck, I thought—"

"I'm okay."

He clasps my face, kissing me hard enough and brief enough that I can't react.

"I love you. I could say it a million times right now." He smiles with relief, his eyes shining. "He's so perfect. I told them you were waking. They're bringing him over now."

My chest pounds at his words. "Is he okay? Is everything…?"

Benjamin's smile is blinding. "He's perfect, I told you. Ten toes, ten fingers."

"Knock knock."

We look to the door, where a nurse is carrying in a small bundle wrapped in a white blanket with blue stripes.

It feels like the moment of truth, the moments that hang just before she sets him in my arms. There are so many questions that momentarily stun me.

Will he look like me? Or like Benjamin?

What will his eyes look like? His nose? His mouth?

Does he have hair?

They all dissipate as soon as his weight settles onto my weak forearms.

This tiny, completely perfect baby is more Benjamin than me. With his chin, the roundness of his eyes, the fairness of his skin, I see his father in him. He has my nose, my shape of fingernails that are so small. He's pink and fragile, his eyes closed in slumber. He has wisps of dark hair, a reflection of both of us.

I'm sure of perfection looking upon him.

"Oh my god," I whisper, struck by delight. I look at Benjamin tearfully. "We made this."

He nods, as enthralled by the baby as I am.

"I want to see you hold him," I say, my voice cracking. I refuse to cry. I hold my arms out carefully, offering our child to my husband. "It's been all I could dream about. You holding him."

Our baby looks even smaller in Benjamin's grasp, not even taking up his full forearm. Benjamin, such a large man, is gently cradling him to his chest, glancing at me to ensure he's doing it right. When he cradles the back of his head, peering down at his child with a smile that could defeat all evil in this world, I'm truly more content than I've ever been in my life.

The sight of them together is all I'll ever need.

"He's so tiny," Benjamin says disbelievingly.

"He looks just like you," I say, softly petting the baby's black curls.

"It's so strange…you know…to see yourself in someone," he says, kind of breathless. "I didn't know I could feel this way." He glances at me.

I nod, understanding him completely. "I know. I feel it too."

"I'm scared. I want to be good…for him."

I clasp Benjamin's cheek and he tilts into my palm, shutting his eyes. "I have no fear."

He inhales as our baby wraps his small fingers around one of his without opening his eyes. We look on with wonder, watching him breathe.

"We have to name him," Benjamin whispers.

I hesitate before speaking, unsure what he'll

think of my suggestion. “What about…Daniel?”

Benjamin’s head snaps up, his eyes wide for a moment at the mention of his twin, the brother he lost as a child to leukemia. I wanted a name that has meaning, and for some reason, we never discussed names. I always suspected he’d want Daniel.

“You…you don’t mind?”

I shake my head, gazing down at our boy. “Daniel seems right.”

When my eyes land back on my husband, I find him staring at me, looking just as unstable as I am. I’ve hardly ever seen him so utterly happy, so emotional. He leans slightly, meeting me halfway, and we kiss softly, slowly, the product of our love between us.

I caress his face, wiping his tears.

“I love you,” he whispers against my lips. “God, I do.”

EPILOGUE

"You're still here?"

Cindy is standing at my office door, her tote bag hanging off her shoulder, no doubt hauling three manuscripts to complete at home. Her timing is impeccable. I'm five minutes late to meet Dimitri downstairs, who will be taking the Scott family to South Carolina in less than an hour.

"I'm moving. I'm moving," I say, packing up my desk.

"Soak up some sun for me? I think I'll have gray hair before I can finally get myself to a beach."

I follow her out of my office. "I'll have a pina colada too, just for you."

"Okay, now you're just rubbing it in."

The building is all but empty now. Even the go-getters have escaped to start their weekend plans. On the way out, Cindy and I shut off the lights and lock the doors. We pack into the stuffy elevator—the a/c unit broke down sometime around lunch—rendering most employees inconvenienced and testy.

"It will be fixed on Monday," Cindy tells me, pulling on the thin scarf wrapped around her neck. It's sweltering outside, but she still dresses as if we work in an igloo. Seeing Dimitri at the curb beside the Escalade, having ditched the usual limo, I part ways with my colleague.

"I know, I know, I'm late," I say by way of greeting.

He opens the door for me. "Everyone's running a bit behind schedule. Benjamin's still in the meeting, so they're holding the jet."

"Doris is waiting for us with Daniel."

"Luggage is on the jet. Everything is in order."

Dimitri merges into rush hour traffic, a magician at missing rough patches and intersections. If there's anyone who knows New York City, it's him.

"How was your vacation, Dimitri?"

"Refreshing. Relaxing. Caught some nice fish."

"And now you have to put up with us."

He smiles. "Don't tell Benjamin, but I quite enjoy it."

"Yeah?"

"Closest thing to family I've got."

I don't need to remind him how important he is in our lives or how much we rely on him. He's Benjamin's most trusted ally, and I know Benjamin would move worlds for him, even if he doesn't vocalize it.

I make a cross over my chest, right where my heart is. "Your secret's safe with me."

The drive to our building, and the penthouse apartment we've made a life in, is short, only blocks away from my office. The front of the building is clustered with reporters and paparazzi starving to lay eyes on my husband, who recently made headlines because of a generous donation to cancer research. Leaving Dimitri in the foyer, I take the elevator up, marveling at how my heart can still leap with anticipation after all this time, at just the thought of laying eyes on my son.

Daniel is content in Doris's arms, but as soon as he sees me, he struggles, wanting to get down. The minute he's on the floor, he's wobbling, unstable but determined to cross the short distance to where I've bent down to retrieve him.

"Come on, baby. You can do it."

Surely having inherited the impressive genetics of his father, Daniel is brilliantly adaptive. He was singing when he spoke his first word, which to our dismay was neither of our names. And he tried to run instead of walking his first steps. He stumbles into my arms, giggling at my excitement.

"You did it!"

I kiss his head, looking up at Doris, who is admiring us from afar. "Thank you so much for watching him."

When I stand, bringing Daniel with me, she throws her hands up.

"This is what I live for. Anytime your babysitter cancels, call me."

Daniel's small hand clenches my dress. "Any new words today?"

"Mama. Mama," he says.

It's not a new one, but one I'm still unused to hearing. He wiggles, trying to be free of my embrace, pointing to his toy on the ground. I watch him go with Doris, admiring the bouncy black curls on the top of his head. His eyes are a soft green color now, only another thing that reminds me of his father.

"You look wonderful. Is that a new dress?"

I run my hands down the length of the cherry-colored number I bought months ago, when I was still attempting to rid myself of baby weight. "You think? It's not too tight?"

"You look sensational as usual, darling. Anyways, there's no time to change. Look at the time." Everyone's on a time clock but me today. I scoop up Daniel, who is mumbling incoherently to his G.I. Joe. Doris throws her purse over her shoulder. "Have fun. Send me pictures, all right? Lots of them. I want to see Danny in the swim trunks I got him."

"Wait, where are you going? I can take you home."

"I'm going with Kevin to interview a new caterer…last minute wedding changes. He told me to tell you to have fun also and be ready to be worked to death."

"You know, I'm beginning to regret maid-of-honor responsibilities. I mean, how many different cakes can you choose from?" I flick my chin toward the elevator doors, arms too full to hug her myself. "I'll let you walk out before me so you don't get mobbed."

She kisses both of us on our cheeks and steps through the doors, which close after a few seconds. Hovering as I wait for the elevator to return, I remember something. On the table in the middle of the foyer, beside a large arrangement of lilies, lies a small hat, with the words *Scott Industries* plastered along the front. I place the cap over his wild curls, smiling along with him.

"You're going to rep Daddy today, yeah?"

Just hearing his father's name, Daniel kicks restlessly, anxiously looking around the room for Benjamin to appear.

"Yeah, Daddy," I hum. "We're gonna go see him now. Let's go see Daddy."

Buckling him into his car seat is a feat, but after I hand him the noisy rattle Benjamin gave him days after his birth, he immediately puts it into his mouth, hardly noticing me strapping him in. I run my fingers through his soft locks, pushing his hair back from his face.

As young as he is, Daniel seems to know the layout of Scott Industries pretty well and the staff even more so. I follow closely behind him as he insists on walking himself onto Benjamin's floor. Tiffany gasps upon seeing him, one of his biggest fans.

"Oh! He's wearing the hat!" Tiffany crows. Daniel has won the heart of every woman in this building. The hat was a gift from her, one she made herself with Benjamin's logo. She gave it to Daniel on his first birthday a few months ago.

Tiffany melts when he grips her index finger. "You can totally tell he was made by the most beautiful people in the world."

I blush.

"Go on in. He's done for the day."

Tiffany retreats into her office to pack up for the

day. I pull open the door, and the minute Daniel catches sight of his father, he's making himself known with a loud exclamation.

Benjamin is seated at his throne of power, the backdrop of Manhattan behind him, along with a colorful sunset. At the happy sound of our son, he shuts his computer, standing with a megawatt smile. It spreads across his face even further at Danny's excitement, the way he bounces, laughing wildly on his way over to him.

"*Danny boy*!" Benjamin kneels, scrunching his tailored three-piece suit. Daniel tumbles into his outstretched arms, and Benjamin lifts him up into the air, placing multiple kisses to his chunky cheek. "Bud, how ya doin'? I like your hat."

"Dada."

I'm transfixed as Benjamin sets him down, murmuring to him, pointing to the mountain of toys set neatly in the play area he had set up in his office just months after Daniel's birth. The entire office, once a daunting, intimidating place, is now childproofed, usually scattered with blocks and musical contraptions. My heart triples in speed when Benjamin rises from his bent position, turning his attention to me. Like a moth to flame, the moment his hands are sliding around my neck and his mouth is against mine, I'm drawn in, melting into his touch.

"You look stunning, baby."

"So do you."

The phone chimes on the desk. I plan to heave his phone into the water if it rings even once this weekend. It's the first vacation we're taking as a family, and I'll have no distractions. With a braced inhale, he presses on the speaker button.

"Yes, Tiffany?"

"I know you're preparing to go, but Alexander is on his way in to give you the documents you requested."

There's a knock on the door, and after one brief look between us, Benjamin crosses the room to greet his brother. When Daniel turned six months old, Alexander finally reached out to Benjamin. It had been over a year since they'd spoken, but when Alexander informed his brother that he'd stopped speaking to his mother upon learning of her treachery, her complete disregard for Benjamin—and the loan she asked for in the hospital room—Benjamin didn't have it in him to hold a grudge. I don't even think he wanted to in the first place. Forgiveness was easy for them. Trying to build a relationship with each other was another thing entirely. That was proving more difficult.

They're trying. That's what matters, I guess.

Benjamin ushers him inside. "Come in."

I see the blond hair first, such a contrast from his adopted brother's black tresses. Alexander sees Daniel and me by the kitchen and stills. We usually steer clear of one another, particularly because we never resolved the misunderstandings between us, and lack the will to do so in respect of Benjamin. Stiff politeness will have to do. I cannot avoid him anymore, not now that he's working for his brother again.

"I'm sorry. I didn't know you were busy."

"It's all right. You have the documents?"

Benjamin asks. Alexander hands him the documents, his gaze fixated on Daniel, who is trying to get his attention.

Alexander bends, brushing his hand through Daniel's hair. "God, he really does look more like Ben every day."

"That's what I say." I cross my arms over my chest, glancing at Benjamin, who sets the work on his desk.

"When do you leave?" Alexander asks me, a notable hitch to his voice. He's being cautious, but his eyes dart away from me.

"Now, actually," Benjamin answers, appearing by my side, sliding a possessive hand across my waist.

Alexander is quick to retreat, smiling apologetically. "I'll get out of your hair then."

"We'll be back in a week. We'll have drinks, yeah?"

Surprised at the invitation, Alexander nods. "Sounds good. Bye, Daniel." He looks at me, for only a moment. "Bye, Darcy. Have a good time."

"Thank you."

He lets himself out, and Benjamin chuckles, shaking his head. "I need to find him a wife, set him up with someone."

"Why?"

"Because he's clearly still hung up on you."

"You're becoming green," I murmur to him, repeating the words he once told me, throwing my arms around his neck.

His smirk warms considerably. "Damn right I am."

"I like that you still get jealous over me."

"I know you do."

"Let's go," I whisper against him excitedly.

"Hell yes. Let's go."

I pick Daniel up, waiting for Benjamin to shut down. He moves fluidly around the office, at ease with his surroundings. I recall first setting sights on him, tumbling over useless words he could easily see through and navigate.

Somewhere inside of me, even then, I hoped. I dreamed.

But how could I have imagined this?

This man is my *husband.* The baby in my arms is ours. Benjamin catches me staring, and the smile he flashes me knows my thoughts.

No doubt he can read them clearly on my face.

I hide nothing from him. Why would I when he's looking at me like this?

***

By the time the jet lands on the tarmac, the sky is dark, the sun having set over the horizon hours ago. The moon is almost full, a beam glowing on the ocean surface. Benjamin's eyes are closed, his head laid back, looking identical to the child tucked in his large arms.

My husband is the man I conjured up in those dreams that felt so far away, so unreachable, but this *is* my reality. I take a quick picture of them together with my cell phone and send it to Doris, who I know will cherish and understand how good it is to see Benjamin this way. The small cottage we will spend this week in is just up ahead, behind a white picket fence and gardens upon gardens of flowers. Tiffany scouted the place almost a month ago and sent me the picture. It wasn't hard to fall in love with the beachside cottage's simplicity.

I comb back Benjamin's hair softly, and his dark eyelashes flutter.

"We're here," I say quietly, not wishing to wake Daniel. I take Daniel from him so he can retrieve the bags with Dimitri, stepping along the pebbled pathway to the stairs leading to a wraparound porch. Right behind me, Benjamin unlocks the door.

The car engine starts, and Dimitri drives away, heading down the road to a separate cabin where he will stay. Benjamin slides through the doorway, carrying every bag we've brought. I giggle, pressing down on my lips when he drops one of them on the wood planks with a grimace. To our relief, the small bundle of energy in my arms doesn't stir whatsoever. I move through the house, checking the doors and finding a kid's room. A crib has been brought in, no doubt because Tiffany thinks of everything.

When Benjamin appears, handing me his bag, I'm able to lay Daniel down to change him into pajamas. His eyes part with reluctance at my movements, but his thumb is in his mouth and he is more than ready for me to settle him down for the night. He yawns against my throat as I rock him soothingly, rubbing my hand over his back.

At home, I play him lullabies, or sometimes "Somewhere Over the Rainbow" to get him to drift off, but I didn't pack anything. Today, I hum the start to the Judy Garland classic, and eventually the vibrations become words. I sing to him, swaying to the imaginary orchestra in my head.

"If happy little blue birds fly, beyond the rainbow…"

I near the end of the song, my own eyelids heavy from listening to the sound of his heartbeat slowing against my chest, and Benjamin is standing in the doorway, leaning against the threshold as if he's been there a while. My cheeks flush slightly at being caught, but the contentment on his face relieves me of embarrassment. I settle Daniel into the crib as gently as I can. Benjamin turns on the monitor, adjusting the microphone volume. I turn to check that he doesn't close the door the entire way, but I don't have to. He's left it ajar.

"I swear there for a moment I thought he was going to wake up." I kick off my heels after we close ourselves off in the bedroom. Furnished with whitewashed furniture and seashells on every surface, the room couldn't resemble the beach more if it tried. Such a distinct difference from our apartment, I admire the fragility, the feminine ambiance of the room while I unzip the back of my dress, dropping it around my ankles.

"He likes his sleep like his mother."

He can't see me gape at the admission since his attention is on unknotting his tie. I can't argue with that.

"Well, you know, I'm actually rather awake right now," I state suggestively, placing the red dress over the chair. Benjamin's gaze is on me, his eyes slanted playfully while he unbuttons his dress shirt, intuitive enough to know what I'm implying.

"Is that so?"

The blush that spreads across my face is betraying. His shirt parts as the last button slips under his fingers, and my mouth dries. I avert my gaze to conceal how easily he can stun me. My bag is open on the dresser, and I take out my nightgown. Suddenly I'm pressed against his front, my thighs easing into the wood drawer.

My eyes meet his in the mirror in front of us.

Sliding his arms under mine, he takes the nightgown and drops it down into the bag. "You won't need that."

A magnificent force of man behind me, I can't help but wonder if I pale in comparison, especially scantily clad, the lasting effects of Daniel's birth marked on my body forever. I should regard the stretch marks as simply another battle wound, one of many, but compared to the towering god-like specimen holding me, it's hard to retain my confidence.

At the way my arms instinctively move to cover my stomach, he catches them, holding my wrists. He only lets them go to nudge my chin, to force me to look at him. He stares down at me, his lips turned up on the corners, bringing out his soft dimples.

"Don't hide from me."

My chuckle lacks weight.

"At every moment of every day, I dream of your body, Darcy. Don't hide it from me."

My arms drop at his command, my limbs becoming like jelly.

"Touch me," he whispers, scaling his hand over

the length of me, his palm gliding over my curves. Stopping at the base of my waist, his fingers tense, gripping down on my hip to spin me. Stumbling, drunk on his proximity and the smell of sea salt that has somehow already scented his skin, I lay my hands upon him, enjoying the way his chest extends and then falls at my charge. I dip my tongue into the crevice between his pecs, my fingers working on removing his belt, multi-tasking at its finest.

He tilts my head to gain access to my mouth. "Christ, I'm already hard and you've barely touched me."

We've both gasped enough air, our lips hovering against each other in anticipation when the sound of the baby monitor picks up a soft whimpering coming from Daniel. We let the breath go on an exhale collectively.

"Damn," he sighs, releasing me. I pick up his dress shirt from the floor and we glance at each other, both wearing disbelieving grins while I work on the buttons. "You look way too good wearing my clothes."

"Pray I can get him down quickly."

When I open on the door, I'm not shocked to find Daniel bouncing on his feet, irritated and wailing now. His tear-streaked cheeks are beginning to splotch red while he waves his arms out for me to pick him up.

"Danny, what's wrong?"

The minute he's in my arms, his cries become hiccups, his head falling exhaustedly onto my shoulder for comfort. I lower the volume to the monitor so the entire house doesn't echo with his cries. Since he doesn't need a change, I take a seat, unbuttoning the shirt enough to see if he's hungry. He latches onto my nipple, his small fingers curling into my chest, which calms the part of me that was nervous it was a nightmare that woke him. With no choice but to stay until he's full and sleepy, I lean back into the chair, planning to lull Danny to sleep.

When his body weight slackens, very carefully, I lift myself out of the chair and set him back into the crib, smiling when his head tilts to the side, his arms stretching up over his head. I escape into the hallway before I make noise and wake him again. With a skip through the bedroom door, I jump to a stop.

Benjamin is asleep in nothing but briefs, his body leaning against the headboard.

Despite the uncomfortable position, he's too peaceful to wake. After a day of work and a night of traveling, plus a baby to care for, sleep is a new luxury for us. I flip the covers back and plant my knee into the mattress, touching Benjamin's thigh.

"Ben, lie down."

His eyes open slowly. "No, I'm awake."

I lay on my side, hugging the pillow. "Let's go to sleep."

He needs little convincing. His large form slides down off the headboard, and after burrowing into the covers, he gravitates toward me, pulling me into his front. My eyes close, encompassed by his warmth, his chin against my shoulder.

"Is he okay?"

I nod, already dozing off. "Sleeping."

I'm not sure how much time has passed when I

awake, but the sky is still dark. The lower part of my body is reacting to the soft tickle of fingertips against my skin, parting open the dress shirt I wore to sleep. I stir, moaning softly while Benjamin covers my breasts, placing kisses along my shoulder.

"I couldn't stop myself," he says, his voice hoarse.

"I don't want you to." I'm primed and ready for him at the drop of a hat, aroused by him in my damn sleep. My thighs are damp with need, my stomach flittering with anticipation as his fingers dive under the waistband of my panties, sliding between my dripping sweet tissues, fondling the tender folds to arouse me further. The soft part of his wrist urges my thigh to widen, so he can travel further down and enter me with a single finger.

"Open up to me," he whispers. "Let me in."

I lift my arm, clasping the back of his head when his lips drift across my cheek languidly, his attention focused elsewhere. My knee bends, my toes digging into the mattress as he retracts his finger to rub my clit, knowing exactly where to coax to make me squirm…to make me desperate.

"*Ben.*"

The last effects of sleep have left me, my skin coated with perspiration as I move with the rhythm of his fingers, which he rotates, piercing me with two and removing them to focus on the small budding of restless nerves.

"That's it. Move with me, baby," he says. "Give into it."

The door in our bedroom which leads straight to

the beach is cracked open, our only form of circulating air. I'm taking up whatever is remaining, my desperation sucking up all the air in the room. It makes our bodies naturally tremble, despite being anything but cold.

"Ah, I'm close," I moan. "I'm so close."

My thighs clamp on his hand the second I feel the jolt in my belly, the stars in my eyes. I let out a soft cry, not realizing there's no need to be quiet since Daniel is a few doors down. Benjamin's arm over my chest holds me in place as I quiver, too weak to resist when he pushes my legs apart from each other, intent on milking the rest of my orgasm to completion. The constant rocking of my hips has made him rise against my back, hard as stone.

I loosen my grip on the comforter when he ceases the sweet torture on my sex, and I'm able to take my first real gasp in minutes, dropping my head back onto him while he slides off my underwear.

Without words, I beckon him for more, my hands sliding against his skin, the muscular thickness of his thighs. It takes no navigating. He's hard enough that his cock with just a tilt of his hips drives into me with ease, the sleek arousal between us lubricant enough to refuse down-time. He grips my shoulder, his teeth sinking into the flesh as he pushes himself through the swollen canal, massaging the tender insides, regenerating the nerves that have exploded.

"Fuck me," I beg him in the darkness, needing more. Always needing more.

And like always, he obliges, kissing me rougher,

driving into me harder. We fuck like dancers who know a choreographed routine by heart. Our bodies are temples we've both explored. We are aware of the pleasures we can receive, of the noises we can coax from each other.

Benjamin easily shifts us both so that I'm flat on my stomach and he's coming at me from behind. Sex is just as important to us as talking, eating, laughing. It has been from the beginning.

The only thing that's changed from back then has been our ability to submit to each other equally, to understand when the other desires the high ground. Benjamin hasn't said it in so many words, but his hands that trap mine on the mattress, his body dominating mine from above, demand my submission, which I offer graciously and abundantly.

I'm his. I want him to always know that.

We own each other.

There is no me without him and no him without me.

***

Benjamin's side of the bed is empty but warm when I wake, my thighs aching. After a few minutes, I'm coherent enough to remember that we're in South Carolina on vacation and I've slept in.

Before I go in search of my husband and son, I haul myself out of bed and into the bathroom for a shower to wash off the scent of sex and brush my teeth. I throw on a black bikini, wrapping a sarong around my hips, and open the bedroom door. I instantly hear seagulls, only loud because the door to the beach cottage is open.

Accompanying the noisy seagulls is child's laughter, a high-pitched wail of joy that can send a shiver throughout my entire body. Stepping out onto the patio, I shield my eyes and spot them under the blazing sun. I can't help but smile, appreciating the sight of Benjamin, free and happy in nature. He's confined to his office, or meetings, and even our city apartment far too often. Seeing him relaxing on the Carolina beach is a sight to behold.

Daniel is throwing around sand, wobbling on his unstable legs, his arms wrapped in thick floatation devices. He's wearing the trunks Doris gave him, and I make a mental note to take a picture of him sometime today to send her. Benjamin's wearing black trunks that conform to his masculine thighs as he chases Daniel, who is now set on playing some form of tag. He won't get far without falling. Benjamin's hands are there when he does and torture him with the wiggling of his fingers, tickling.

Daniel's fit of laughter can probably be heard all the way where Dimitri is staying.

"Having fun, are we?"

Their heads turn at the same time at my amused question. Benjamin gasps, grabbing Daniel's hand. "Look! It's Mommy!"

"*Mama*!" Daniel shrieks as Benjamin helps him to me. He trips twice but eventually makes it, stretching on his toes for me to pick him up. When he's in my arms, Benjamin leans in, pressing his mouth to mine with a smile.

"Good morning."

I blush, unable to help myself. "Yes…it is."

***

Laid out against Benjamin, tucked between his thighs, I regard the book on my lap with zero intent to actually decipher the sentences. Daniel is on the blanket as well, playing with a soaked-through teddy bear. He's completely immersed in it, speaking gibberish, his own private language. An umbrella shields us from the scalding sun, and to fight off the heat spells, we have the water. Daniel splashed Benjamin the entire time, to my everlasting amusement.

Benjamin has a hand rested on my thigh, tracing the beauty marks absentmindedly. *"Voglio quel libro,"* he murmurs in Italian. *I want that book.*

I repeat it, without half the grace as him, a fluent speaker, rubbing his thighs. There are still water droplets on them from when he jumped in the water a few minutes go. "Fitting for me."

"Very fitting."

Utilizing my husband's vast knowledge of languages, I listen to him speak, picking up on his teachings as best I can. He's a patient tutor. I lean against his chest, humming contentedly when he presses his lips to my cheek, his tenderness disarming, but not at all unlike him.

"Je t'aime," I tell him. *I love you.*

He squeezes me closer. *"Tu es ma vie, mon amour."*

I tilt to him with a pleased smile. "I like that one."

He grins. "I thought you would."

We move together simultaneously, our mouths magnets, drawn to each other, impossible to resist. We touch lightly, apprehensively, lingering in the closeness, that moment of anticipation before he swoops in and takes me swiftly. My heart still leaps at his attention, as it has since I first laid eyes on him. My mouth naturally slackens so his tongue can slip through, and taste me, drink me in. We only pull apart when Daniel knocks into my legs with a wild laugh, oddly pleased to have interrupted his parents' intimacy. It's contagious—his innocence, his unfaltering joy of the world.

We've hardly been witness to that kind of life. Now that we have him, it's easy to fall victim to bliss.

"Danny boy, you want some help?" Benjamin asks exuberantly, shifting back into the sand so he can stand. He settles down onto the edge of the blanket, accepting the bucket Daniel is holding out.

For a brief moment, I'm transported to the moment I laid eyes on my husband. Benjamin Scott was cocky, arrogant…untouchable. I was mesmerized the second I saw him. I was still a frightened, naïve girl on the run from a dangerous past. There was no one. I was alone. I can still see myself sitting on a bench in Central Park, trying to imagine the lives of the people aimlessly trotting by me. Oh, how I envied them. The life they had could never be reached for me.

I never saw a life with friends, family. I couldn't

anticipate a son, never dreamed of a husband. I knew better than to envision that. I knew it would be impossible.

But it wasn't.

I owe my entire life to Benjamin. He's saved me. He's given me everything a person could possibly give someone. He's changed who he is for me. He learned to love for me, and it's more than I could have ever asked for. He knows I'm grateful. He knows how much I love him, how much I rely on him.

We've finally grown up.

Our pasts make it easy to be parents. We love as we wished to be loved.

I stare, transfixed by my boys. Benjamin's emerald eyes dart up from the mess of a sandcastle, a breathlessly unmarred smile consuming the greater portion of his face when he finds me watching them. His smile dissipates into something else, something *more*. He reaches out his hand, motioning for me to join them.

I stand with a shaky exhale, emotional as I walk toward my happily ever after.

The End

Acknowledgements

This journey with Benjamin and Darcy has been a wild, amazing one, and there are so many people to thank. I wish I could get everyone, but I'm sure I'll miss out on a bunch of you. If so, you can call me and murder me later.

This trilogy began on Wattpad, which I updated chapter by chapter over the course of two years. In that time, Consumed by You, won a Watty Award for Best New Adult Romance and passed over the infamous million reads line, even eventually reaching five million before it was passed on to Limitless Publishing.

To Wattpad and every person who followed along with the journey and supported me along the way, I thank you from the bottom of my heart. I have an endless supply of love for you, and I hope this ending gives you the satisfaction you wanted. I hope I've done these characters justice and provided them with an ending to their chapter most would wish for in their own lives. I've met some of the honest-to-God greatest people on this site, and I'll always be grateful for the friendships and opportunities I've gotten from the decision to join and begin writing. A special shout-out to Adrienne Stinson, a Wattpad friend, who was the first person to pre-order Consumed by You before I'd even announced it. That was a great feeling for me and I'll never forget it. You're freaking awesome.

To Limitless and my team—Lydia, Bella, Dixie—you guys are rock stars. I've said it before.

I'll say it a hundred more times. To my editor, Felicia Sullivan, thank you for your dedication and attention to detail throughout this whole process. You've helped these stories immensely and I'm so pleased with the final result.

Deranged Doctors Design has made all three of The Consumed Series covers, and I've been blown away every time I've been presented with them. I'm so grateful for their hard work.

To my friends and family, ones near and far, thank you for all your support. You know I love you. Nanny, Tata & Papa Abuelo, your belief in me pushes me to be better every day and I wouldn't be where I am without you.

And lastly, to the people this book is dedicated to, Mom and Tatyana, a million thank you's wouldn't suffice. These books wouldn't have been made without you both. You guys are my biggest supporters, who nurture my crazy ideas and I love you for it.

About the Author

Her life consumed by Wattpad, Scottish Romances, and Walt Disney World, Alicia Marino attempts to find a piece of magic in everything. She blames (and owes) Jane Austen for igniting her desire to search for evidence of that forever type of love. Settled in not-so-sunny Florida and a classic introvert, she thrives off of rainy days paired with a good book and a glass of whiskey.

Facebook:
https://www.facebook.com/alicia.marino.5

Twitter:
https://twitter.com/aliciamarino10/

Instagram:
https://www.instagram.com/aliciamarino/

Wattpad:
https://www.wattpad.com/user/AliciaMarino

Join our Reader Group on Facebook and don't miss out on meeting our authors and entering epic giveaways!

Limitless Reading

Where reading a book is your first step to becoming limitless...

Limitless Publishing Reader Group

Join today! *"Where reading a book is your first step to becoming limitless..."*

https://www.facebook.com/groups/LimitlessReading/

Printed in Poland
by Amazon Fulfillment
Poland Sp. z o.o., Wrocław